Trust No One

Shai Renae

Snakes may smile,

But they still bite.

Can I trust,

Who's closes to me.

Who can I trust?

Mostly my day ones.

Watching my back,

Looking over my

Shoulder.

I can see the love

fading away.

Cause hate reveals

Their true colors.

I'm moving forward,

No matter who's

with me or against me.

Because trust is word,

I would use to determine

Who's going to stay

Chapter 1

It's Friday night of April 20th, 2012. The sky is completely dark, cloudy, and not a star shining in sight. The rain slams against the window, sounding like little pellets being shot against a metal wall. The night feels calm and the streets are quiet. A night where a person likes to sit on a porch and watch the rain or lay in bed sleep.

Sitting in her room, nine-year-old Alani Bennett is playing with her toys. As she was playing, a flash of lightning, lights up the sky in a bright blue. Then suddenly, thunder crashes making the whole house shake from it sound. Frighten, Alani runs to her mother's room. She bust open the door seeing her mother Katrina and her boyfriend Joey jump out the bed naked out of fear. They quickly put some clothes, while Alani stood there in shock.

"What are you and Joey doing?" Alani asked.

"Well…hun…uhh, we were practicing naked yoga like your Aunt Candice." Answered her mother Katrina. "Why don't you go back to your room until I come get you."

"Ok." Alani walked back to her room feeling confused. She hoped her mom wasn't turning them like Aunt Candice.

"Naked yoga, I never heard of anybody doing that shit." Said Joey.

"Well she seen my sister do it so, I had to make her think I was doing the same."

"Why couldn't you say sex."

"NO! she a kid, she don't understand that stuff yet."

"Nowadays kids do."

"Well, not mine."

Once they had their clothes on, they went downstairs to sit in the living room. Katrina turned on the tv and they both started to watch Law and Order SUV. Joey's phone has been going off non-stop. He had 5 missed calls and 7 text messages. Once again, his phone started ringing.

"What, I'm busy." Joey answered annoyed.

"Where you at man. I been trying to call you. Some dudes ran in your house. They looking for you. Damion and Patrick got shot and they're dead and I ran out and escaped. Right now, I'm hiding out. Until I know for sure they're gone." Said Mikey panting.

"Ok. Wherever you at, I'll meet you there." Joey quickly hung up and rushed out the door.

Sitting there confused, Katrina got up and looked out the window. She seen a car pull up and two masked people jump out with guns. Three gunshots rang out and Joey collapsed. She quickly ran upstairs and rushed into Alani's room. She told her to hide under the bed and wait until she comes and gets her.

Katrina ran downstairs to find the two masked people ransacking her house. One of the masked people grabbed her and threw her to the floor. They place a gun to her head and asked where Joey's stash was because Austin got tired of waiting for it. She told them many times that she didn't know. They ran up the steps and searched in every room. Alani hid in a secret compartment. Joey built it for her behind her headboard with an inside lock for her, when she wanted a secret hiding place.

They search all over her room even underneath her bed. When she heard the footsteps leave the room, she let out a sigh. She sat in there and waited for Katrina to come but, she heard screaming and then two gunshots after. She kept waiting.

Five minutes went by and still silence. She unlatched the lock and crept out her room. She walked downstairs and peaked through the railing of the stairs. She saw her mother slowly crawling towards her cell phone across the room with a trail of blood behind her. Alani rushed downstairs and ran towards her mother with fear.

"Lani go get some help; I can't move any further." Her mother said struggling to breathe.

"I don't want to leave you here mommy. I can't go outside without you watching me." Said Alani with a face full of tears.

"It's Ok sweetheart, this is an emergency. Now go get some help."

Alani ran outside and searched for a house with it's porch light still on. That's a rule Katrina taught her when it came to emergencies. The rule is if the porch light is not on, assume they are asleep. She walked by every house down the block and the porch lights were off, and some were on but, later turned off. She found help at the last house on the street. She repeatedly banged on the door until someone answered. A lady opened the door with a face covered in green pasty face mask, a robe, and a bonnet. You can tell she was a black woman from the skin tone on her hands.

"Can I use your phone. I don't have one and my mommy needs help." Alani said panicking.

"Ok, honey come inside." Said the woman, escorting Alani into house.

"Thank you." Alani said.

The woman gave Alani her cell phone and sat next to her. Alani dialed 911 and the operator answered.

"911, what's your emergency?" Asked the operator.

"My mom have been shot." Said Alani crying.

"Ok, honey where's your mother?"

"She laying on the floor bleeding."

"Is she still breathing?"

"I don't know, I'm at somebody else's house to use their phone."

"Honey, I need you to stay there right now. Can you give me your address."

"Ok, 163 Formore Drive. That all I know."

"That's alright hun. I think we will be able to pull up you address. Ok were sending help now. I need you stay on the phone until I say to hang up."

"Ok."

After the operator gave Alani the ok to hang up, the woman turned the tv and switch the channel to cartoons. She tried to entertain Alani by giving her snacks and sharing stories and telling her mommy is going to alright. Alani started to feel a little better. The lady even told jokes to make Alani laugh. They was having a good time until someone knocked on the door.

"Hi mam, I'm detective Baron. I was told there was a child here that made a call from this location."

"Yes." Said the lady in confusion. "How the hell you know she was here?"

"We traced the call from the phone GPS to pinpoint the child's location. We'll take care of the child from here. Can we have your name in case we have contact of the child's relative and for our case file records.

"Jenette Reeds. Sweetheart someone here for you."

"Thank you for your cooperation Ms. Reeds."

Alani rushed to the door thinking that her mom was there. Instead she was greeted by Detective Baron and two officers.

"Hi honey, my name is Detective Baron, we're going to take you with us. Until we can reach one of your family members."

"Is my mommy ok?" Asked Alani worried.

"She ok for now. We'll let you know tomorrow if she gets better. Right now, we need to get you to a safe place."

Alani rode in the back of the detective's car. She stared out the window and looked up at the sky in silence. She wondered if her mom made through and wondering where's Alani.

They pulled up at a building southside of Tampa Bay, Florida. It's a shelter for orphans, runaways, and lost children. There's even a few children that was saved from kidnappings and human trafficking rings. If any of these children's relatives don't claimed them within a year, they will be sent to foster homes.

Detective Baron placed Alani in a room by herself away from the other children. Just in case she was able to contact her family members right away. She made sure Alani was comfortable and one of the shelter staff fed her dinner. Once she fell asleep, the detective drove back to her office. She spent countless hours looking for her relatives. Once she typed in the last name of the Katrina's name from her driving license they found in her purse in her bedroom, she knew she hit the jackpot. An old case file popped up; she knew who to call.

Day after the incident………

Detective Baron returned to her office at 10am after a long night of searching on who to call. She finally has contact of one of Alani's relatives. After making the call she waited for the family member to come. Three hours later a woman walks into the office. She's dark skinned, 5'5 in height, has a 28" in weave that is in two plats. She wore a black mesh shirt and dark brown pasties stuck on each breast, blue denim mini shorts and black flip flops. She also wore a white flower headband on her head.

"Hello, you must be Alani's aunt. correct?" Said Detective Baron.

"Yes, where's my niece?" Asked Candice.

"She's staying at our Children For Hope shelter."

"What the hell is she doing in there?"

"She made a call last night saying that her mother was shot. Apparently, the call came from a neighbor's cell phone close by.

"OH MY GOD!!!! Is my sister ok?"

"Unfortunately, I'm sorry to inform you that your sister, died on the scene. That's why your niece was placed in our shelter last night."

Taken aback by the answer Candice excused herself and walked out to the empty hallway. She fell to ground with her arms wrapped around her and cried. Her and Katrina were close, even after what happened to them in the past. The pain from knowing that her sister is gone felt worse than the abuse endure in the past. Now Candice feels she has no one to go when she's in need. After spending 20 minutes crying alone, she wiped her tears and walk back into the detective's office. Detective Baron gave Candice some tissues and pulled out a file.

"I just made a call to tell the staff back at the shelter to have someone to bring your niece here at the station. Now that's out the way, I'm going to start working on your sister's case. The only information I can give right now, is that we think it might have been an attempt robbery. We do know for sure is that there was a second person there was shot at the scene. That victim, identity cannot be release due to the fact that they are a shooting victim and their protected for their safety."

"Ok." Said Candice holding back tears.

"If we get any more information, we'll let you know."

Then came a knock on the door. "Detective the child has arrived."

"Bring her in."

Alani slowly walked in the office. Candice quickly turned around and seen Alani. She smiled and jumped out the chair to give her a hug. Alani was smiling to see someone she knew but, felt disappointed it wasn't her mother. Once they got the ok to leave, Candice took Alani to her house. When they arrived,

Candice took Alani to her guest room. The room was the only clean room in the house.

"This house use to be your grandparents house until they died from their car accident. Then it got passed down to me and your mother. This room used to be your mother's room. I pretty much kept out of it since. I guess this will be your room now. I'll be in my room if you need me."

Candice walked away sad. Alani wanted to know if her mother was ok. But that's answer she's still going to have to wait for.

Dinnertime came around and the best that Candice can do is order food. She wasn't the type that always cooked and cleaned. She spends most of days high, drunk, and meditating with crystals and sage. Candice called Alani downstairs to eat. Once she got downstairs, not to her surprise Candice was naked. On the coffee table was a large box of pepperoni pizza, cheese fries, BBQ wings and a large vegan pizza for herself. They sat at the coffee table and started eating. Alani finally build up the courage to ask about her mother.

"Is my mommy ok?"

Candice slowly put down her food and took a deep breath. She waved over Alani to sit on the couch. She turned her head for a second to try to hold back the tears. She grabbed her hand gripped it tight.

"Sweetie, your mommy…...(sigh) She's in heaven right now with the angels. But she looking down at you right now smiling, knowing that you're ok." Answered Candice with a cracking voice and tears.

Alani sat there in silence. She didn't what to say or how to feel. She just sat there, silent. She slid off the couch and went back to the table to finish eating. Candice can tell that was a shock to her. Once they were done, Alani ran upstairs and slammed the door. Candice knew that the news is starting to hit her.

She sat on the couch and pulled a bottle Jack Daniels out from underneath the couch cushions. Then she pulled a small box that was Velcro underneath the coffee table and pulled a blunt and a lighter. She sat in her corner with her crystals, lit the sage and the blunt, took one big shot of the liquor, and one big puff of the blunt. She closed her eyes and tried to let her mind drift her away from the pain. Meanwhile Alani is upstairs in bed hugging the pillow tightly and crying while saying "Why did you have to go mommy."

Chapter 2

It's been a week since Katrina died. Both Alani and Candice sat in the front row of the funeral in tears, hugging each other. It was an open casket, so it was even more painful for them endure. Once the service was ending, they closed the casket. Candice broke down in tears, screaming. A few family members walked over to her and tried to console her. Every family member and friend was there. The whole room sobbed as they try to listen to the preacher. Some couldn't handle the site of Katrina being in the casket lifeless. The preacher welcome Candice up to speak. She walked up slowly to the microphone, took a deep breath, and wiped her tears.

"First of all, I would like to thank everyone for coming." She took a long pause. "My sister was everything to me. She was there during my hard times and checked up on me during my good times. A piece of me left when I got the news saying she was gone......" Candice started to cry but, she took she took a breath and kept going. "I'm going to miss her and what truly hurts the most, is that her daughter has to grow up without her mother. Alani was her world and she love her to pieces. She never let that little girl out of her sight. Katrina was loved by everybody. She is the light we're going to miss around us. We love you and we going to miss you sis." Candice walked back to her seat and continued to hold Alani. As the choir sang, five guys from the family plus Mikey carried her casket to the hearse.

On the way there, they all sat in silence in the limo. Not one word came out from neither family member. Their hearts are so broken, to the point where no one can speak. When they arrive at the burial site, Candice's stomach started to turn as they placed the casket on the straps. Everyone was given a rose drop on the casket. As the preacher says the final words, the casket drops lower. When he was finished, the attendees threw the flowers in the grave site. Candice collapsed and was crying so hysterically; she almost fell in the grave site. Alani stood there frozen with the rose in her hand. She closed her eyes and thought of the memories she had with her mother. It was the only thing that kept her alive at this moment. She walked over to her grave site to drop the rose she watch it fall and hit the casket below with a couple tear drops with it.

Everyone met back at the church for the repast. Some sat down and ate, while others mingled with each other. Candice seen Mikey with his head down, with his hands over his face and a hood over his head. She walked over to him and placed her hand on his shoulder. He looked up to see who it was and then looked back down.

"This wouldn't have happened if Joey would have followed through." Said Mikey shaking his head.

"What do you mean?" Asked Candice.

He got up and wrapped his arm around Candice's shoulder and they both walk outside.

"We were supposed to meet up with Austin with the stash but, Joey didn't answer his phone. So, Austin got tired and sent his people out for us."

"What the stash?"

"It's some vape oil he made called the paralyzer. It's oil from granddaddy purple and Cyclo a muscle relaxer. He got from his dad cause his dad stopped using them three months from his car accident, when his muscle spasms stopped. Anyway, he mixed those together in pan then he crushes some the KO Kush and adds it to the oil, and he lets it sit for a week. We tried it to do a test run a week later. Man, that's some good shit. We were stuck on the couch for hours. We even ordered food and the delivery driver had to come in and put our food on the table." He giggled, while shaking his head.

"We been hyping it up to Austin for weeks. He wasn't with it at first but then he got tired of us begging so, he tried a sample of it, and he been wanting a piece of it since. Damn, we could have been making good money with Austin in on it."

"So, my sister died over fucking vaping oil?" Candice said angrily.

"It wasn't supposed to go down that. If Joey answered his phone, we have avoided it." Said Mikey trying to reassure her.

"Blame the dead man." Candice said rolling her eyes.

"Actually, he's alive. He was shot three times, once in the shoulder and twice in the back."

"Where is he?"

"He's at home resting and recovering. He moved to his other house in the back woods. He needed a place to hide out from Austin."

"Has he heard the news about my sister?"

"Yeah, I told him. He didn't take that very well. He started drinking and smoking heavily. He became all depressed now. He asked about Alani too, but I couldn't tell him much so, he started to freak out. A matter fact, I need to go check on him make sure he don't do anything stupid."

"Ok, well let him know Alani ok."

Mikey waved good-bye as he walked down the street and got in his car. After he drove off, Candice went back in and started to mingling with the family members and friends. Alani is playing it tag with her cousins and few friends from school. Everyone started to have a good time dancing and using this time to catch up with each other. Each person took turns talking on the mic, remembering Katrina. The day went from being sad to a day of joy about Katrina.

One by one each person were heading out to go home. Once everyone said their good-byes to each other, they all went home. Candice grabbed Alani and they walked over to the car. Alani got in the backseat and Candice got in the driver's seat. She looked in the rearview mirror and seen Alani staring out the window. Tears were rolling down Alani's cheeks as she look at the church. Candice tried to hold back the tears while she started the car. But when she started driving tears started falling down her cheeks.

Meanwhile at Joey's house..........

Mikey pulled up and parked on the side of Joey's house. Joey lived in a house in the backwoods where no one would know there is even a house there. Mikey walked in the house and found Joey drunk and passed out on the living room floor, hugging a picture of Katrina and Alani on his phone. Mikey tapped Joey, scaring him out of his sleep.

"Did you finish this whole bottle of D'usse by yourself?" Asked Mikey.

Joey sat up in silence. The room was spinning so fast that he couldn't think of an answer. Mikey shook his head and sat on the couch. He rolled a blunt, lit it, and starting smoking it. He put his head down and took a minute to think. Then he looked up and seen Joey struggling to get up. He walked over to Joey, helped him up and put him on the couch.

"Let me get a hit bro." Said Joey mumbled.

Mikey gave the blunt to Joey. He was so drunk; he had a hard time finding his mouth. Mikey snatched it back cause Joey had it backwards and started burning his face. Joey leaned sideways on the couch and laid his head on the arm rest. Suddenly he started to cry again.

"To make you feel better…. Alani is alive." Said Mikey trying to lighten the mood.

Joey quickly sat up "She's alive?"

"Yeah from what I heard, she's staying with Candice."

Joey felt a little relived, but at the same time angry with himself. If he wouldn't have spent so much time with Katrina; he would have remembered to meet up with Austin.

"This is all my fault; I should have reminded myself about that day. I haven't seen Katrina in a week, and I thought I could squeeze some time in. Plus, I haven't spent much time with Alani, and I felt like a deadbeat."

"How you going to feel like a deadbeat if you don't know if she's yours?"

"As I watched grow up until now, she starting to look like me."

"So, why don't you get custody of her since you're so sure she's yours?"

"I can't, we haven't done a DNA test yet. I been so focus on coming up with a product for Austin to like, I haven't gotten around to that."

"But ain't you on the birth certificate."

"No, me and Devin were supposed to do a DNA test to see who gets to sign the birth certificate. But Devin refused to do one because he found out me and Katrina were fucking around. So, he thought she was mine. Then he went ghost afterwards."

"Wait, I thought they broke up. That why ya'll messing with each other."

"No, Devin was cheating too. I told her she can do better, and we started doing little shit and she started to have feelings for me. It ended up being tit for tat in her world."

"So, are you going to do one?"

"Yeah. Now that she's getting older, it's time for her to know now that Katrina gone."

"Yeah. How you going to do that without Candice trying to jump on it?"

"She has to agree to it. Candice not much of a good guardian for Alani anyway, with the way she is. I hope she doesn't get upset and try to keep Alani away from me, cause her and Katrina were close."

"Well good luck tomorrow man."

"Thanks, I'm going to need it."

Chapter 3

It's Saturday afternoon of May 5, 2012. Mother's Day is two weeks away. This year is going to be the worse for Candice. Not only she lost her mother seven years ago, but she lost her sister who was also became a mother with Alani. She tried her best to keep Alani's mind off of it. After Candice had her meditation time. She cleaned her house for the first time in weeks and she attempted to make lunch. She made cheesy broccoli rice casserole with grilled chicken on the side for Alani. Even though she's a vegan, she made some adjustments for Alani so that she can eat without being picky.

Alani was playing with her toys that she got from home. Going back home was traumatizing for Alani. She started to have nightmares about that night after visiting the house. They had to clean sweep the house and grabbed everything for storage so, the landlord can put the house on the market. Since everyone knows about what happened, no one wants to rent there.

She heard Candice call her down for lunch. So, she dropped her barbies and rushed downstairs. She had a bowl of the broccoli rice with chicken on top sitting on the coffee table for Alani to eat. Alani sat down and started eating. Alani slowly chewed the food trying not to show the face of disgust. Candice could tell she didn't like it by the way she was eating. Candice got up and went to the kitchen to taste her food. As Candice is in the kitchen, there was a knock on the door.

Alani got up and looked out the window and noticed a light-skinned skinny guy standing by the door. He had on a red hoodie with the hood over his head. His locs were peeking through his hood. She couldn't see his face didn't know who he was, so she called out to Candice.

"Aunt Candice there's someone at the door!" Alani yelled.

Candice came rushing out the kitchen and to the door. She looked out the window of the door and saw the man with the red hoodie sitting on her porch. She unlocked the door and opened it slowly and left it cracked open.

"Who the fuck are you?" She said through the crack of the door.

The man jumped up in fear and quickly turned around. Candice knew who it was and open the door to invite him in while giving him the look of disgust. They sat on the couch and Candice wrapped the cover around her.

"When are you going to start wearing clothes?" Asked Joey looking away.

"When people start minding their business about what I do in my house." Candice snapped back.

"JOEY!!!" Shouted Alani as she peaked out the kitchen. She rushed and jumped on his lap.

"Hey pretty girl. How are you?" Said Joey with a smile on his face.

"Good. I'm going back to school next month. I can't wait, cause I miss my friends. I got to see three of my best friends at my mom's funeral. How come I didn't see you there?"

"The doctor said I had to stay home and rest."

"Did the bad people who hurt my mommy, hurt you?"

Joey sat there in silence. He didn't know what to say afterward. All he can think about was that night.

"Yes, Hun they did. He went to go get help just like you did." Said Candice answering for him. "You want to go upstairs to your room while I talk to Joey about something important."

"Ok." She said skipping up the steps.

"So, what are you here for?" Asked Candice.

"It's about Alani, I think she's my daughter and I want to do a DNA test." Joey answered.

"What makes you think that?"

"I started to noticed as she got older, she's starting to look like me."

Joey handed Candice two photos. One from when he was nine and Alani's current school picture. Candice can see some of the resemblance from comparing the two photos. Then she handed him back the photos.

"I guess I'll grab some Q-tips from upstairs."

Candice walked upstairs; Joey turned his head. He couldn't bare seeing Candice naked anymore. He misses Katrina, her smile, her body, her laugh, everything about her. He can feel himself tearing up again. Candice came back downstairs with Q-tip in a zip lock bag.

"It already done for you. I had to tell Alani her dentist called, and they need a sample to check her teeth."

"Ok, thanks Candice."

"Anything else?"

"I'm going to go upstairs say good-bye to Alani."

Joey went upstairs and into Alani's room. As he went in Candice pulled out her phone.

She texted: *Joey's alive, he's here at my house but, he's about to leave soon. He came to get a sample from Alani to do a DNA test. What should I do?*

A text notification went off on her phone.

It replied: *I thought you said he was dead you know what, let him go. Let me know when them results come back.*

Why do you need to know that.

Because I know the motherfucker is going come back around more often if she his.

Ok, I'll keep tabs on him. I'm going to need something in return.

Like what?

I want to come see me today. I haven't seen you in weeks.

Alright, I'll see if I could squeeze in some time.

Candice rushed upstairs and into the bathroom. Joey shouted out saying he was leaving, and Candice shouted back okay. She turned on her flat iron and sprayed her hair with heat protected spray. She took a quick shower and spent an hour in a half straighten her bra length black hair. Her phone went off showing she got a text message saying he will be there in the next hour. She walked to Alani's room to see what she was doing. Alani was watching her favorite show My Little Pony. She closed the door quietly and went back downstairs. She sat on the couch and waited until she gets a call.

Three hours later she gets a knock on the door. She looked at the time and it was almost 8pm. She jumped up and looked in mirror next to the door. She made sure her hair, her lace bra, and lace panties looked good. She opened the door and there staring was Austin.

"Hey sexy, I see you got on something special for me." Said Austin impressed.

"As always." Candice said smiling.

Austin walked in and sat on the couch. Candice walked to the kitchen to grab a bottle of José Cuervo, two glasses, and a sprite as a mixer. She came back sat next to Austin. She poured two shots of the liquor and gave one to Austin.

"Cheers to my new informant." Said Austin taking the shot with Candice.

He gave her a new Gucci purse that was filled with stacks of money. Her eyes widened and her jaw dropped. Austin looked at her, smiling as if he got her wrapped around his finger. He lifted her head up by his finger and leaned in closer to her.

"There will be plenty more of that sweetheart. Just give me more of the information I want." Said Austin slyly.

He leaned in for a kiss. He kissed her hard and long and Candice melted. She gripped his shirt and pulled him closer but, he gently nudge her off of him. She snapped out of the moment and made herself a drink. The two sat on the couch and watch what was on tv. Austin phone started to ring. He got up and walked to the kitchen. After 20 minutes he came back out upset.

"Everything alright?" Asked Candice.

"Yeah, it's Devin he did some dumb shit without paying any attention." Said Austin brushing it off.

They continue to drink and chill out until Candice started to get a buzz.

"You alright?" Asked Austin.

"I'm good, I just need to smoke right now." Candice answered.

She reached for the box that underneath the coffee table. She pulled out a pack of rolling papers and a little baggie of what's left of her weed. Austin grabbed the weed out of her hand and put it back in the box. He pulled out a big bag of the new product he was selling out of his pocket.

"Try this." He said handing her the bag.

She wasn't sure about it first but, she grabbed it anyway and started breaking it down on the paper. Once she had a good amount, she rolled up the blunt. She lit and took a big puff. Then she passed to Austin. He took one puff as he watch Candice slowly fade. Then he passed it back to Candice. She took another puff and gave back to Austin.

"What's in this?" She asked.

"It's confidential." He answered

"What do you mean it's confidential?"

"It's something new I'm testing out. Since I don't got the other product I wanted to put in."

"Oh, ok."

They sat on the couch high and drunk. Candice looked over at Austin and got turned on. His caramel skin glowed against the living room light. His hair is a shiny black with lose curls pulled up into a man bun. The around the sides and back is in a low cut, with the front of his hair lined up perfectly. He has a thin mustache and goatee. He wore a crisp clean white tee shirt, black sweatpants, fresh white socks, and black slides both Nike. She lean on his shoulder and started rubbing his arm. She loved the artwork of tattoos on his arms. He looked over at her and smiled. She looked up and seen him smiling. They both what they had in mind.

She got up while still holding his arm and took him upstairs. As they walked past, she peaked into Alani's room and Alani was passed out asleep. They entered in Candice's room and Candice shoved Austin on the bed. She climb on top of him and started kissing and licking his neck. She slid her hands down his pants and rubbed him

39

until he got hard. Then he flipped Candice over and ripped her panties off. He licked her from her belly button to her neck, as she dug her fingernails in his back causing her to scratch his back. He inserted his erected penis in her and stroked slowly. It felt so good that Candice tried to stay quiet by biting her lip. He moved faster and harder which made Candice moan louder, waking up Alani in the other room. His phone went off, so he flipped Candice over and shoved her face in the pillow.

Still going he reached for his phone on the nightstand and seen there was a text message. He opened it up and there was a picture of Joey walking into the Northfield Clinic. The text underneath said: *Got him and we found where he hiding at.*

Austin texted back: *good, drop the location.*

He tossed his phone on the nightstand and flipped Candice over on her side and kept going until they reach the climax. They flopped on the bed and laid there. In the next room, Alani lays in her bed staring at the ceiling. Awaken by the noise in Candice room, She can't seem to go back to sleep. Hours goes by and she still awake. It's 12:45am and the only noise she hears now is her TV. She tried to shut her eyes to force herself back to sleep. She heard her door crack open, she thought it was Candice checking on her. Slowly, she opened her eyes and turned her head to Austin standing by her bed smiling.

"Wow, who knew you would be as pretty as your mother." Said Austin touching her face softly.

Alani laid there staring at him. She didn't know what to say. Then Austin sat on the bed and started rubbing her leg. She kicked his arm away with force. He laid down next to her and started running his fingers through her lose curly hair. Alani laid there frozen, afraid of what he's going to do to her.

He whispered in her ear. "Don't worry, I won't hurt you. I wouldn't touch a little girl your age. I have a daughter your age, it wouldn't be right if I did. But I'll wait until your 18.... maybe 16 since I'm not a patience person. And Joey, if we ever find out if he is or not your father, he can't protect you cause he's afraid he will end up like your mommy. Don't worry Uncle Austin will take care you, like a niece until you blow out those 16 candles, then I'll make you a woman and after that you belong to me. So, be ready by then."

He kissed her on the cheek, got up and walked out the room. Alani sat up and started thinking. Is Joey really her father or is Austin just messing with her? And what did he mean by making her a woman and becoming his? There was a lot going through Alani head. She didn't know how to feel. Instead she stayed awake afraid of what he's going to do next. She jumped up and moved her dresser in front of her door. Using that as security, Alani got back into bed, she closed her eyes again. With the words from Austin running through her head. She is not looking forward for

her sixteenth birthday.

Six Years Later

Chapter 4

A few things has happened in the past six years. Austin forgave Joey, but Mikey warned Joey that there's a hidden agenda behind it. Cause Austin not the one who will forgive so easily. Also, Candice allowed Austin to move in once they got into a relationship; after finding out that Joey is Alani's father. Which made Alani installed a top lock for her bedroom door, to keep Austin from coming in her room every night with a reminder.

It's Thursday morning of September 6, 2018. Alani is now 15 years old. She's three months away from her sixteenth birthday. Alani starts high school today. Rising out of bed, after the sound of her alarm, Alani is not ready for the day. She spent all night finding an outfit and picking a hairstyle from hairstylists' Instagram. She got up out of bed and went to the bathroom. She turn on the shower, got undressed from her pajamas, put a shower cap on and jumped in. The hot water felt good on her skin. It feels like it's washing away all of her pain and fears. She washed up and turned off the shower. She stepped out to see Austin in the bathroom looking in the mirror.

"Oh, I thought you were Candice. That's why I'm in here. Since we're both in here I figure I get a sneak peek of what about to get in three months." He said running his hand up her upper thigh.

Alani brushed past and he pulled on her causing to fall off. He looked at her smiling and licked his lips.

"Fucking perv." Alani mumbled as she rushed out the bathroom and to her room and slammed the door.

She locked the top lock on her door and got dressed. She looked in the mirror to see if her outfit looked right. She's wearing a white knitted long sleeve sweater top off the shoulders, with front tucked in her light blue denim skinny jeans with the rips in the front, and her diamond studded sandals. She put on her gold

14k diamond necklace with her mom name in a heart; Joey gave her that necklace for her thirteenth birthday.

She unwrapped her hair from her scarf. Her fell down softly little passed her shoulders. It was silky straight, smooth, and soft. She had Candice straighten her hair the night before. She parted her hair to the side and laid down her edges. The to put two clips on the side saying baby girl. Then she applied some white eyeshadow, black eyeliner making cat eyes, and mascara. She looked at the time and seen it was almost 7:40am.

"Shit." She said as she threw on her gold hoop earrings, grabbed her lip gloss, bookbag, her cell phone and her keys.

She rushed downstairs and into the kitchen. In there, Candice was cooking breakfast while Austin sat at the table rolling a blunt and counting money. Candice turned around and seen Alani. She smiled while holding back tears.

"Awe look at my high schooler." She said giving Alani a hug. "You look just like your mother from hair down to your clothes."

"Really?" Alani said confusion.

"Yeah, your mom use to dress like that in high school. I'll show you a picture after school."

They all ate at the table until Austin got a call Devin saying that got to meet up with Sammie to seal the deal. He kissed Candice and as he kissing her, he looked Alani with a smirk. Alani was grossed out and looked at her phone. Candice sat there with a huge smile on her face. Once Alani finished eating, her and Candice got in the car and drove her to school. As they're driving from Northside of Tampa Bay to Southside Tampa Bay, Alani can see all of the teens walking to school. Some had on uniforms, some dressed how they liked. They pull up in front of Linton High School. Alani looked around to see if any of her best friends were around. Then Candice caught her off guard.

"I know your mom would be excited to see her little girl growing up and going to high school. Oh, The stories she would have told you about her high school days." Said Candice smiling. "Well have a good day." They both hug each other, and Candice started to cry. Alani got out and wave good-bye and headed into the building.

There at the entrance is the principal, vice principal, and the guidance counselor. They were welcoming students as they entered the door. There is a line to grab schedules for their classes. Alani was two people behind. After them she is up next.

"Hello, I'm Principal Simmons. What your name and grade?"

"Alani Bennett, 9th grade."

The principal search through the pile of papers in the 9th grade folder. She found Alani's schedule and handed over to her. Attach was a small piece of paper that had her locker number and combination numbers.

"Thank you." Said Alani

"You're welcome and Welcome to Linton High." Said Principal Simmons.

She walked down the hall and to her locker. She tried the combination on her locker. She was able to get it open and she looked at her schedule to see what class she had first. She has Algebra 1 for first period. So, she grabbed everything out her bookbag placed them in her locker except one notebook, her pens, and personal stuff. As she closed her locker door, she heard someone call her name. She looked around and seen Shadaya running towards her and giving her a hug.

"Bitch I been looking all over for you." Said Shadaya with excitement. Then she started singing, dancing, and twerking, "We in high school, we in high school, eh, eh, eh."

"Girl, everything is a celebration with you." Alani giggled and shaking her head.

"Yeeaah, you know afterschool we going to roll a blunt, drink some drank and get fucked up." She starts singing again. "Cause we in high school, we in high school."

"What class you got first period?" Asked Alani.

"Algebra 1 with Mr. Clemons." Shadaya answered.

"Me too."

"Aww shit, we going to be cutting up together, cheating off, each other, and whispering about bitches."

"Whispering?"

"Yeah, you know we can't be talking out loud or we going be fighting."

"Oh yeah, I can't be doing that. I already got enough at home."

"Is your aunt's boyfriend still trying be creep?"

"Yeah. I might have to go to your house for a minute. Cause I don't want him creeping up on me asking if I met anyone."

"I don't blame you. Girl why you think I said we getting fucked up."

They both laughed and as the bell rang, they went to their first period class. When they walked in, they seen there were open desk in the back. So, they rushed to the two back seats that were in the corner of the classroom. They turned their seat facing each other. Ten minutes later Daisy walks in with a guy next to her. She sees Alani and Shadaya sitting in the corner. She and the guy walks over to them and grabs the two desks close by and move them over to the girls.

"Hey Daisy, who's this?" Said Shadaya looking him up and down smiling.

"This my cousin Princeton. He just moved from New York." Daisy answer.

Princeton is 5'8, brown skin, honey brown eyes, light mustache and goatee, hair cut short around but with lose curls at the top that falls in his face. Alani stared as if she was bitten by the love bug. When he smiled, he the perfect set of teeth and dimples.

"These are my friends Shadaya and Alani."

"Well you can sit in front of us so we can have somebody cute to look at. Right Alani....... ALANI!!!!"

"Uuuuhhh, yeah."

Shadaya leaned over and whispered in Alani's ear. "You ok. Cause you look like you over here drooling."

"I'm good."

The teacher walked in and introduce himself.

"Hello, class I'm Clemons. And I'll be your AP Algebra 1 teacher for the year."

Fast forward to the end of the day.......

Alani got a text message from Shadaya saying to meet them at the back of the school. She walked to the exit that led to the back of the school. Standing in the group by the bleachers is, Shadaya, Daisy, Kelcie, Princeton, and Aaron.

"Aight since everybody here. Where, we chilling at?" Aaron asked.

"We can't go to my house. My mom at work and she locked up her liquor cabinet." Said Shadaya.

"We can't go to my house or Jamie's because my mom is home and Jamie in Miami for business, so he says." Said Kelcie.

"We can go to my house. I'll see if my dad is home." Daisy offered.

Daisy texted her dad: *Dad, are you home? If not is it ok for my friends to come over?*

"You sure you want to chill at your dad's house? There's a lot of work moving in and out of there now that my dad added his workload there." Princeton said concerned.

"Yeah, unless you want to see Alani's aunt walk around the house naked." Said Daisy trying to convince him.

Shadaya asked Alani "Does she still do that?"

"Yeah, I thought she will stop doing that now that she has a boyfriend." Alani replied.

Daisy got a text message back: *Yeah princess, you can invite your friends over. I will be in the basement most of the time.*

Daisy rolled her eyes. She hated when he called her that. They started walking to Daisy's house which is three blocks from the school. But first they stopped at Jamie's house. Kelcie dug through her purse and pulled out her keys. She unlocked the door and walked in. Two minutes later she walks out three bottles in a plastic bag. In it is two bottles of Patron and one bottle of Hennessey.

"How the hell you get a key?" Asked Shadaya.

"He gave it to me before he left. He said if I needed anything, I had to get it myself."

Lucky, they didn't have to walked that far from Jamie house. He lived on Bryers St which is a block away from Daisy's house on Kilmore St. Once they got there, they in and walked straight up the steps. Surprisingly, the house was clean. Since Princeton and his parents moved here, they been living with Daisy's Dad until they found a house to live in. Most of time his mom has been keeping the house clean.

"Dad, I'm home will be upstairs in my room." Shouted Daisy.

They all sat in Daisy's room and Daisy used the Bluetooth from her phone to connect to her Bluetooth speaker and turned on her Pandora App. Daisy turned the speaker up to the max. Aaron got up and stuffed the sheet under the door. Aaron jumped on the bed and sat in the corner of the wall by the headboard. He waved over Daisy over and she jumped on the bed he is and the two started cuddling.

"Aaron, while ya'll over there boo loving, get the sparking. I know you got some." Said Shadaya snapping her fingers.

Aaron rolled his eyes and reached over the bed and grabbed his bookbag. He pulled out a packet with two blunts rolled already. Daisy grabbed her lighter out the drawer in the nightstand. She gave it Aaron and he sparked one blunt, took a puff and passed to Daisy. While they started the rotation, Kelcie pulled out the bottles of liquor.

"Wait, how do have liquor and no cups?" Shadaya wondered.

"I'll go grab some and a chaser." Daisy said getting up from the bed.

She passed the blunt to Shadaya and walked out the room. Shadaya took two puffs before passing to Alani who is sitting next to her on the small white bedroom couch. By the time Daisy came back, Princeton was passing it to Kelcie. Kelcie took a puff and passed to

Aaron. Next, she grabbed the cups from Daisy and poured everyone a shot.

"Let's take a shot for the start of the new school year. Henny for the boys, Patron for girls." As she said while passing them out.

They all cheered and took the shots. An hour went by and they continued to smoke and drink. There was a couples of songs they started dancing to. Then Daisy asked what they wanted to do. Aaron suggest they should play never have I ever. But in this game, they would take shots if did.

"Aight, never have I ever, skipped class to fuck in the lower level bathroom."

Daisy, Aaron, and Shadaya took a shot.

"My turn." Daisy jumped in. "Never have I ever, stole money from my parents."

Shadaya and Kelcie took a shot.

Shadaya's turn. "Ok, I got a good one. Never have I ever, snuck into the boy locker room.

All the girls took a shot.

Alani next. "Ok, I guess it's my turn, Never have I never snuck out the house for a party."

They all took a shot.

Princeton turn. "Never have I ever, gave head."

Shadaya, Kelcie, Daisy, and Aaron took a shot.

"Yo, I don't want to play this game anymore. I'm going to be drunk after this." Shadaya laughed.

"You ain't the only one." Said Kelcie feeling the buzz.

"Alani, you and Princeton are the only good kids cause ya'll only took one shot since the game started." Said Daisy.

"Daisy you know how my parents are." Said Princeton with a side eye.

"Let's get back to the game cause it's my turn." Kelcie interrupted. "Never have I ever, drunk text an ex."

"What the fuck man." Shadaya said before taking a shot.

"Maybe you should stop doing shit." Daisy laughed.

"Let's switch this up because my bro Princeton and Alani took the least shots. We going them drunk. They going to have race see who can take ten shots in two minutes. Then throw them in the closet for seven minutes of heaven." Aaron laughed.

"Babe don't do that to my cousin. Now you're doing too much." Said Daisy getting upset.

"It's cool babe, I was just joking."

"I'm wit it." Said Princeton.

The stopped and looked at Princeton. Alani can feel her face turn red, while Daisy sat there in shock.

"Well, let pour some shots." Said Aaron grabbing both bottles of Hennessey and Patron.

He poured some shots in the cups everyone had. He set the timer for 2 minutes. Princeton and Alani cheered each other and smiled. Aaron started the timer and they both started taking shots. Alani and Princeton are tied until Princeton started moving fast. Before the timer hit under one minute Princeton finished the 10th shot. While Alani just finished behind him. Once they were done, Aaron set the timer for 7 minutes. Alani and Princeton went inside Daisy's closet. Aaron started the timer. They inside looking down at the floor. They were shy at first then Princeton started the conversation. They were having a good conversation until Shadaya shouted.

"Turn the music down, I can't hear them moaning." Everyone laughed even Alani and Princeton laughed so hard they couldn't even stay in the closet for the whole 7 minutes.

Alani said she had to go to the bathroom. Daisy told her where to go and Alani walked out.

"So, what did ya'll do?" Asked Shadaya curiously.

"Nothing really, we just talk. I like her, I think I want to get to know her more." Answered Princeton.

Shadaya, Kelcie, Aaron and Daisy looked at each other with smiles on their face.

In the bathroom……

After Alani was finished going to the bathroom. She looked in the mirror. She couldn't stop smiling after the seven minutes in heaven. Just getting to know Princeton made her like him even more. She wish Shadaya didn't make it awkward. She walked out the bathroom with her head down, not trying to show the smile on her face. She heard someone come up the steps. So, she kept walking. Then she looked up to see who it was.

He smiled. "I guessed you know where my house is huh. Is Candice here somewhere?"

"No, I came here with Da…."

Then it came to her in a flashback. *(Let me see if my dad is home….)*

And that's when it clicked. Daisy is Austin's daughter.

"What were you about to say?" Austin asked.

"Daisy is your daughter?"

"Yeah, why are you one of her friends?"

"Yeah." Then something came up in Alani's mind. "By the way, I just meet your nephew Princeton and I'm starting to like him." She smiled hoping it will keep Austin away from her. Then she proceeded to walked towards Daisy's bedroom door and walked in. Austin face went from smile straight to a frown.

Chapter 5

The next day everyone showed up to school with a hangover. The hours felt like it was dragging by in slow motion. Time finally started to move faster right after lunchtime. That's when everybody started to sober up. When the school day ended, everyone walked home, while Candice picked up Alani. On the ride home, Candice is on the phone with one of her friends. All they talk about is how their relationships going. Alani tried to ignore the conversation the whole ride. When they got to the house, Alani hurried out the car and into the house. She knew Austin is home because his car is parked in the driveway.

She rushed upstairs and into her room. She curled up under the covers and started dozing away until she got a text message. She looked at her phone and it is from Princeton.

I wanted to tell you earlier that I'm sorry if I made you uncomfortable yesterday. It was the alcohol talking not me lol.

Lol, it's ok. I had fun anyways.

If you're comfortable, would you like to go out for a date?

I like that, what time and day?

Tomorrow at 7.

That will work.

Cool, then it's set.

Alani snuggled under her sheets again. She closed her eyes and started to dream about her and Princeton's life in the future.

After her five hour nap, it's now 8:00pm. She got up and checked her phone. She had three missed calls from Shadaya and a text message saying *call me back.* She clicked on Shadaya's name and it started ringing.

"You called?" Alani asked.

"Yeah, who else would have called you." Shadaya replied with a smart remark. "Anyway, I called to tell you that Charlie called me."

"Charlie? You mean Aaron's friend, the Charlie that been chasing after you since 3rd grade."

"Yeah, that weirdo. We been talking and he said him and Aaron are throwing a party next Friday. He said we need to come cause everyone is going be there. So, you in?"

"Yeah I'm in. What time?"

"He said 7,8ish depending on when people start showing up."

"Cool, I guess we're hitting the mall after school Thursday."

"Let's go tomorrow at 5."

"Ugh, I don't about tomorrow I have a date."

"With who? I need know cause you can't drop out of my plans for some dude."

"You can guess who."

"Bitch, y'all met yesterday. Well you was staring him down at school and he did say he wanted to get to know you more."

Alani smile with excitement. "He really said that?"

"Yup, so you'll be ready by noon?"

"Why so early?"

"Cause you need an outfit for the party and your date duh. You got to be fresh if he's taking you out." She said laughing.

"Ok I'll be ready by noon."

They both hung up and Alani went downstairs. She passed Austin who is sitting on the couch smoking. He gave her the evil eye as she walked pass. She rolled her eyes as she walked in the kitchen. She seen on the table that there is a bucket of chicken, mashed potatoes, and gravy, with biscuits and wedges from KFC. She made herself a plate and headed back upstairs. Thinking that she had to be up early; she ate, watch some TV until she made herself go to sleep by 11pm.

Back at Joey's......

Joey is on his couch watching TV enjoying a beer. He has a lot on his mind. From thinking about Katrina missing her little girl grow up to Alani's 16th birthday coming up to having Austin wanting his product again so he can make the money to get a surprise for Alani. He texted Mikey to see if he should bring up his product again or drop it and create a new one. He got a text message back:

I think you should sell it yourself. Bring it up again just going create the same situation again, but this time with Alani. We don't need Austin to push new products anymore. He can't be trusted.

Joey texted back: *What do you mean he can't be trusted.*

Mikey replied: *You forgot how he forgave you out of nowhere. I told before the motherfucker can't be trusted. He got something up his sleeve and it ain't good. Another reason is that he let you live. I know*

69

people like him made sure you die. I don't know man; I think his

plans has Alani involved.

What make you think Alani is involved?

I think he trying to get you where it's going to hurt the most

just in case shit go left again. Remember Joey, he knows Alani is

your daughter and you know how he moves.

Joey sat there and started thinking. How can he push this product on his own and who can he connect with? He got to find someone who he can trust and that Mikey cool with. He start going through a list of people. Jerome? No, Kanan, Nah he run his mouth too much. He kept thinking maybe he'll have to wait on Mikey for this one. He's good when comes to picking people cause he can read them like a book.

He got up and went to the kitchen to grab another two more beers. He sat back down on the couch and place the beers on the table. Suddenly, he hears a knock on the door. He got up and rushed to the door. He looked through the peep hole and seen it was Austin and Devin. He let a long sigh and opened the door.

"What's up I haven't heard from you in while." Said Austin with a smile.

"Nothing much, just chillin."

Austin and Devin walked right past Joey and sat on his couch. Austin grabbed one of Joey's beers that was on the table and cracked it open.

"What brings you here" Asked Joey with an unhappy look.

"I came to tell you something. See my family from New York moved here into town and I found out he met Alani."

"So, is it something I should worry about?"

"Yeah, the reason why he moved here is because he was involved in this gang called the Red Bandits. Those motherfuckers are dangerous cause they move quiet. Next thing you know you either in some deep shit or dead. Long story short he still got contact with them. So, keep an eye on him and tell your daughter to be careful."

"Aight, let her know."

"Oh, another thing about the stash we were supposed to make a deal on, is it still on table?"

Joey face turned white and he can feel his soul leave his body. Mikey said not to bring it up or make a deal with it. Then he notice Devin with his arm around his shoulder and a gun on his back. He left with no choice, but to agree.

"Yeah, it still on the table." Joey said nervously.

"Good. Let me know when we could make official. Thanks for the hospitality." said Austin walking out smiling.

Joey watched Austin pull off from the house. He slammed the door and sat on the couch shaking his head. How is he going to explain to Mikey. Then started to have a panic attack cause he know if don't follow through again he's dead for sure. He just going to have to be upfront with Mikey. They have a choice to either make the deal and be stuck with Austin or come up with a whole new plan.

Chapter 6

Alani jumped up out of her sleep from the sound of her alarm. She looked at the time it was 11am. She got up and picked a simple outfit. She pulled out her black leggings, plain white tee shirt, and a black leather jacket. She went to the bathroom to shower. As soon as reached for the door, Austin opened the door. He walked out smiling and then Candice came behind holding his arm smiling. Gross out by what she assumed, Alani jumped in and took a quick shower.

Once she was done, she went back to her room and got dressed. It is 11:40 and she texted Shadaya saying she's ready. She pulled her hair up into a bun and threw on her sneakers. She picked up her furry mini bookbag. She threw in her lip gloss, her wallet, and her keys. She looked at her phone and Shadaya texted back I'm about to pulled up. Alani rushed downstairs and in the kitchen. She grabbed a water and some doughnuts and walked towards the door.

"Where you going this early?" Asked Candice.

"To the mall with Shadaya."

"Oh, ok. Be home before 8."

"I'll be home by 5."

Alani heard the horn go off and walked out. Outside is Shadaya in an all-black 2018 Range Rover. Alani jumped in and looked around.

"Who's car you steal?"

"My dad's, he back in town. He let me borrow it cause trying to be a father again." Said Shadaya rolling her eyes and pulling off.

"Oh, this is nice. You didn't tell me you got your license."

"No, I still got my permit. I was waiting until you got yours."

"I wasn't getting mine until my 16th birthday. Cause then I can have it in my hands that day instead of waiting."

"Makes sense."

While the girls on their way to mall, Joey left a text message to Alani......

Joey drove to Mikey house. He lived in one of the newly built condos Downtown of Tampa bay. He looked at his phone again...no reply. He got out and buzzed the number to Mikey's apartment.

"Who is it?"

"It Joey, I got bad news to tell you."

"Aight."

Mikey buzzed him in, and Joey walked through the doors and the lobby. He took the elevator up to the third floor. He walked to

Mikey's apartment and knocked on the door. Mikey opened the door and let him in. Joey sat on the couch with his head down.

"What the bad news?" Mikey asked sitting next to him.

"Austin and Devin showed up at my house last night."

"What the motherfucker want?"

"He came to tell me to warn Alani about his nephew."

"Why would he do that?"

"I don't know. He said his nephew in some gang called the Red Bandits and he told me to keep Alani away from him or she going end up in some shit."

"Ok, He couldn't tell her that himself. Something don't sound right."

"That not the bad news. He asked about the stash and Devin had me at gunpoint. I couldn't say no so, the deal back on the table."

"FUCK!!!! I knew he was up to something the day he squash the beef. Damn. Now he going use Alani over your head."

"Why do you feel like Alani going to be involved in this?"

"How many times do I got to fucking remind you. She's your daughter. He could do anything to her. Especially with Candice fucking with him, who knows what her dumbass is going allow what he wants to do. You know what, we just going have to come up with new product. Something Austin won't get his hands on. We just going have to connect with a new people and come with something that wasn't done before."

"I was thinking the same thing."

He looked at his phone and seen he got a text message from Alani:

Ok, can we talk about tomorrow. I doing something today.

He texted back: *Alright. I'll see you tomorrow but get dress I'll pick up around 4.*

Ok.

Back at Candice's.......

Alani is getting ready for her date. Shadaya picked out a short white dress that has lace in the mid-section and sleeves. She also pick out some white wedge shoes. Alani curled her hair and applied some makeup. She got a text message from Princeton asking where her address. She sent him the location and he text back saying he's on his way. She looked at the time and it 7:05pm. Impress on how she looked, she grabbed her mini bookbag with her stuff still in it. She walked downstairs and sat on the couch waiting for Princeton to come.

"Well you look pretty, where you going now?" Asked Candice with a smile.

"A date."

"How long is going to be cause, it's right around curfew"

"8:30ish"

"Ok, well have fun and if you're not home after 10, I'm calling the police."

"I'll be home by then."

Candice gave her hug and went upstairs. Then Austin came walking through the door.

"What you all dressed up for?" Asked Austin.

"I got a date." Said Alani not looking at him.

"With who?"

Then came a knock on the door. Alani got up and opened the door. Princeton is standing at the door with big bouquet of red roses.

"Pretty roses for a pretty girl." Said Princeton with a smile.

"Thank you."

Austin shouted. "HEY NEPHEW."

"HEY UNC. You know my uncle?"

"Yeah, long story." She said rolling her eyes.

They got in a limo Princeton's dad rented for them. They rode to this restaurant Downtown of Tampa Bay. It's called Chaffron Moran. It's the most expensive and fanciest restaurant in town. When they walked in, they were escorted to the back of the restaurant. There was a space there filled with flowers and romantic music. Alani is in awe; she is so amazed with how this date is going so far.

"Wow, you can really impress a girl on a first date." Said Alani amazed.

"For you, you're the only girl I want to impress." Princeton said pulling out a chair.

The two ordered they food and enjoyed the rest of dinner for the night. After the romantic date, Princeton has another thing up his sleeve. The two took a ride to the beach. There sitting on the blanket is more roses, a white teddy bear, a bottle of Cruzan Mango Rum, and a grey box.

"I thought I end the night at the beach and relax from the world for a moment."

Alani couldn't stop smiling the whole time. They sat and talked some more. Then the rum made them feeling comfortable to where they cuddled on the blanket. Then the two kissed, Alani felt the spark between them. They stopped and look at each other and smiled. Alani looked at the time on her phone, it's 9:40.

"I have to go back home before my aunt has a panic attack." Alani got up quickly.

"Ok, Cinderella." He laughed. "There's one thing I want to give you."

He picked up the grey box and opened it. Inside is a sterling silver 5 carat diamond bracelet. Alani stood there in shock about to tear up. He placed the bracelet on her wrist and kissed her hand. They both walked back to the limo to take Alani home.

When Alani arrived, she gave Princeton a kiss and walked to the house. She waved goodbye and proceeded to walk in. She closed the door behind her and rush upstairs to her room. She jumped backwards on her bed and started to giggle. Then she received a text message from Princeton: *I just wanted to tell you good night and you looked beautiful tonight.*

She texted: *Thank you, you look handsome and goodnight. I had fun tonight I enjoyed my time with you.*

Chapter 7

It Sunday morning and the sun shined so bright; Alani pulled the covers over her head. Five minutes later, she woken up to a missed call from Shadaya. She called back and no answer. So, she assume she was doing something else. Alani got and went downstairs to the kitchen to make herself a bowl of cereal. After she made herself some and went back upstairs with it to her room. She turned on the TV and started eating and chilling out in her room. She looked at the time and it was 4pm. She jumped up and quickly got dress forgetting that she was suppose be ready for Joey to pick her up. She rushed downstairs and as soon as she opened the door Joey was pulling up.

She got in the car and they drove off. He took her to Dairy Queen Southside of Tampa Bay. He knows that been her favorite place since she was younger, and she still loves it. She will always get Fudge Brownie Blizzard. Once they got there, she got her blizzard, they sat at the table that is underneath a tree five feet away from the building.

"Who gave that bracelet?" Joey asked noticing her wrist.

"Princeton gave it to me." She said showing it off smiling.

"Speaking of Princeton, his uncle stopped by my house. He wanted me to tell you be careful of his nephew."

"Why couldn't he tell me himself."

"Who knows, but he told me the reason Princeton moved down here is because he was part of a gang in New York called the Red Bandits. The they the most dangerous. He said he still got connections with them."

"Dad, Austin probably saying some bullshit...."

"Alani."

"Sorry, I mean he could be saying anything. Princeton not a bad guy.... I hope."

"I want you to watch out for him. He may be sweet to you, but he's Austin's nephew. Who knows what he has up his sleeve."

"Yeah."

After their daddy daughter time. Joey took Alani back home. They gave each other a hug and she walk into the house. She went to her room and texted Shadaya telling her to come over. Ten minutes later, Shadaya knocked on her door. She got up and opened the door.

"Hey, I tried calling you back, but you didn't answer."

"I was with Mr. Handsome."

"Oh, ok make sense. I need tell you about my date."

Shadaya jumped on the bed and laid on her stomach. She gazed at Alani with her hands holding her head. "Go on." She said.

"Oh my god, it was the best date I ever went on." Alani said excitedly. "First we got in a limo."

"A limo?"

"Yes, a limo and then we went to Chaffron Moran, and he took me to the beach, and we sat there, chilled and drank. And look at this bear and I don't know what to do with these roses. And then all of sudden we kissed, but that's wasn't the best part of the night. He brought me this bracelet."

Then, she hold out her arm showing the bracelet on her wrist. Shadaya's eyes widen as she seen the bracelet glisten in the sunlight in her room. Shadaya jumped up and touched with amazement.

"Did he go to Jared or kiss you with Kay?" Then they both laughed.

"Well he kissed me so…. I go with Kay."

"He must really like you if he did all that. I don't know he might just be a keeper."

"I hope so." Said Alani sitting on the bed looking down.

"What makes you say that."

"My dad came to pick me up to tell to be careful with Princeton. Cause Austin came to his house to warn him."

"That shit don't sound right. Why couldn't he tell you himself?"

"That's what I said. Then my says that he was a part of a gang called the Red Bandits."

"Red Bandits, who the hell they?"

"Some gang in New York. He said they're the most dangerous gang. Princeton moved down here, but he still has connections to them."

"What kind of connections?"

"Don't know, he didn't say too much. I mean what am I supposed to do? I like him, I really do, but I'm not sure if I should believe what I hear."

"I think you should hear out from Princeton before you make a choice. I like him too; he seem like he's going to be good for you. He talked about getting to know you more and went all out for ya'll first date. Don't give up on it just because of a rumor. Remember, this came from Austin."

"Yeah, you right. I'll ask Princeton about tomorrow. See what he has to say."

Standing outside Alani's door.......

Austin listened to every to word they said. He can feel himself He getting angry, but he calmed down and thought of something new. He will have to talk to Princeton before Alani does. He walked to the bedroom and grabbed his phone and quickly texted Princeton.

I need to talk to you tomorrow. Meet me Devin's house by 5.

Princeton texted back. *Ok.*

Now he got to figure out how to convince Princeton to make

him stay away from her.

Chapter 8

Princeton woke up after his after school nap. He had two hours of sleep last night. He been up thinking about his uncle's text message all night. He hope something bad didn't happened again to where he has to leave town again. He just got comfortable in his new school, met a girl he genuinely likes and just live a normal teenage life without having to be caged in house under surveillance. He looked at his phone from Alani:

Hey, do you have time to talk today?

Princeton texted back: *Yeah, I have time. I got meet with my uncle today at 5 so, it will be after that.*

Ok, I will see you after that ☺

Now Alani wants to talk to him. He rolled out of bed and went to the bathroom. He jumped in the shower and stood there holding to the wall. Twenty minutes go by and there's a knock on the door.

"Princeton, you been the shower long enough sweetheart." Said Dana.

Princeton snapped out of his thoughts, wash up and got out. He went into his room and got dress. He threw on a black tee shirt, black sweatpants, and black sneakers. He grabbed his phone and keys and went downstairs into the kitchen. His mother Dana is cooking lunch.

"Ma, can I borrow your car. I have meet Uncle Austin somewhere." Asked Princeton.

Dana asked. "Why can't he pick up or have your father take you there?"

"He's in the middle of something at Devin's and dad doing stuff."

"I'll take you, but Ima have some words for him."

5 o'clock comes around and Princeton on his way to Devin's. They drove ten minutes outside of Tampa Bay and pulled up into Collins Townhomes which is a gated community. They got buzzed in and she stopped in front of Devin's. Outside waiting was Austin.

"Thanks, sis, for dropping him off."

"Mmhm, whatever you got going on there, there better not be a curl out place when come back and the next time you want him to meet you somewhere, you come pick him up."

"He'll be fine sis; I'll have him back in an hour."

"Ok, and you don't get into any trouble."

"I won't." Said Princeton with a side eye.

She pulled off and the two went into the house. He told Princeton sit at the table with Devin and Jamie. Now he's feeling more nervous.

"Well nephew, I brought you hear to warn you about Alani." Austin said sitting down at the table.

"What about her?" Asked Princeton.

"Well...... she not the girl that you see. She can't be trusted. Alani can be sneaky at times. She could be playing you right now. Her dad is using her to figure out my next move. What I'm trying to say is, she helping her dad get ahead of the game. Since he can't can be too obvious."

Princeton looked at him confused. He still doesn't get the point Austin trying to make. Then he thought to himself, *Alani wouldn't do that...... Would she?*

"I'm saying be careful nephew, she will put you in a position where the only choice is to be buried in the ground. Her playing along with you is a set up to take me down. Right boys."

Devin and Jamie shook their head in agreement.

"You need to stick with Daisy, she watching all her moves." Devin jumped in.

"Yeah try and stay away from her." Jamie warned.

After an hour of trying to convince him to stay away from Alani, Princeton has mixed emotions. He felt he should leave her alone, but something didn't sit right with him. Instead, he texted Alani saying to meet her at the Crescent Park so they can have their talk.

At Crescent Park, Princeton is waiting for Alani. She shows up still dressed from her meeting with Joey. Both gave each other a smile and a hug. They sat down on a park bench under a tree.

"So, what do you want to talk about?" Asked Princeton hoping it's good.

"My dad came to pick me up today and basically told me to stay away from you."

"Why?"

"Your uncle told my dad that you use to be part of a gang and you got in trouble so, you had to move down here, but you still got connections to them."

"What gang?"

"Red Bandits."

"I was never part of Red Bandits, but my dad and uncle were in it. The only reason we moved down here is to get out of New York. Because my uncle screwed them out of money. So, they started coming after my dad cause they couldn't get to my uncle."

"Oh."

"I don't know what he told me is true, but he said not to trust you because your helping your dad take down my uncle."

"Oh, now that a lie. I don't what's going on most of time. And how am I helping my dad take him down, I barely get to see him because of Austin."

"Well, we know enough about each other. Even if it's true it would been brought up."

"Yeah I agree."

Since they were out already. They decided to go for some burgers at Burger World. They found a table to sit at and order burgers and milkshakes. They started to enjoy the time they had together. They completely forgot about what lies Austin said to them. It even brought them closer. After they were done, Princeton decided to walk Alani home. It was a forty minute walk from Southside to Northside of Tampa Bay. As they walked Princeton held Alani's hand and they talked about their past life. Princeton feels like he knows a lot about Alani and vice versa for her.

When they arrived at Candice's house......

Alani noticed Austin's car wasn't in the driveway. 'Thank god.' She said in her head. When they got to the door, they stopped. They smiled at each other and hugged. Alani went to walk in, but she turned around and asked if Princeton wanted to come in just in case Austin shows up.

Princeton said "Sure."

Alani called out for Candice but there was no answer. She pulled out her phone and called her.

"Are you home?" Asked Alani.

"No, I'm at a party with Austin. Why is there something wrong?" Candice responded with fear.

"No, everything good here."

"Alright, as long as you're ok."

They both hung up. Alani offered Princeton a drink. As she went in the kitchen, she grabbed two cans of sprite out the fridge.

They went upstairs and into Alani's room. He was looked around until Alani turned on the tv. She switch the channel to whatever Princeton wants to watch. He choose to watch animal planet. Luckily, his favorite show The Vet Life was on and it was a marathon. One thing that Princeton has planned in life is that if he doesn't become an NFL player, he wants to become a veterinarian and create a shelter for abused animals. He told Alani that it's a second dream of his since he was a kid.

They both are watching the show and getting into it. The show made Alani change her mind about being a celebrity stylist. The two decided to cuddle up once they got comfortable. They were so into the show, Alani looked at the time and it was 9pm.

"It getting kinda late. You should head home, I don't want you get in trouble by your parents."

"Yeah it is kinda late. I don't think I would get in trouble much. My dad probably out with my uncle too and my mom might have gone with him to keep an eye on him and his drinking."

They both got up and walked downstairs to the front door. He went to give her a hug and a kiss goodbye. He walked out until he got to the end of the driveway then he stopped. He turned around and looked to see Alani still standing by the door. He walked back to the door and kissed her again. The two went back upstairs to her room. They kept kissing on her bed until he stopped. Then he sat up on the bed and gazed in silence.

"What's wrong?" Alani asked with concern.

"I don't know, feel like I'm moving things too fast for you." He answered scooting away.

"I don't feel like things are moving fast. We talk so much I feel like I already know you enough. If you feel like are things are moving too fast, we could be friends."

"Nah, I like you too much to be friends. I met a few girls, where I get close to someone and they stopped talking to me cause they wasn't ready. Plus, they thought I was weird because I'm quiet."

"I'm lucky to have friends like your cousin, Shadaya, and Kelcie. Cause it was the same for me."

"I see we are a lot alike." They both laughed.

"Yeah I don't see us lasting as friends for too long."

"I agree." Then he thought about it. "Sooo, what do you think?"

"Think about what?"

"Us making it official."

"I think we should make official, why wait."

They looked at each other and smiled, then went back to kissing. Since they feel the adults are going to be out all night, they had the whole house to themselves. No rules, no watching their every movement, and no curfew (for Princeton anyway). They could invite a few people over to hang out, but they use the time to cuddle, kiss, and not be virgins anymore.

As the night went on, Candice came in house by herself. She is upset because Austin didn't want to come home with her and decided to go to a strip club with his brother and his friends. She stomp upstairs and slammed her bedroom. She got undress and threw on some sweatpants and a large tee shirt. She wrapped her hair in a scarf and was about to lay down, but instead she went to check Alani's room. She turned the knob and the door opened. She was shocked because her door was unlocked.

She looked inside and seen two people sleeping in Alani's bed. She tiptoed in to get a closer look. She pulled the covers back slightly and seen Princeton's face. Known that she done something like this in the past, she looked under the bed and found all of both Alani's and Princeton's clothing. Already agitated, she just let it go for the night and would have a talk with Alani in the morning.

She went back in her room and laid down. Thoughts were going through her head. She felt like she let her sister down in taking care of Alani and how would she explain this to Joey and Austin without them holding grudges against each other again. Should she even mention it at all. Instead she going to keep it a secret until it comes out from somewhere. She got a text saying he was going to stay at his house for the night. She threw her phone at the wall and went to sleep.

Chapter 9

Candice sat around and waited for Alani to come home school. To make things worse on Alani she went to school late because her and Princeton overslept. She went into the kitchen, poured herself a cup of Jack Daniels and starting drinking it straight. She paced back and forth as she was getting upset. Then she heard the door open and shut closed. Alani walked in the kitchen noticing Candice is sitting at the table angry.

"Sit." Said Candice with anger.

Alani sat down on the chair across from Candice at the table.

"You want to tell me what was going on last night."

Alani's heart sank. She knows what Candice was talking about.

"We didn't do anything."

"Explain to me why I found clothes under your bed."

"We changed into pajamas."

"Ok, but if you changed, why was the clothes hidden under your bed?"

"I don't know. It probably got kicked under there."

"Why was Princeton sleeping in your bed?"

"He came over to study for a test and he got tired and fell asleep. Geez why are you so upset over something that didn't happened."

"Alani, I'm not stupid. I've done stuff like this at your age and mother too. I'm calling the clinic today to see if they have anything this week. I'm putting you on birth control."

"That's not fair!!!" Alani yelled.

Candice yelled back. "I don't care, I don't want you to end up like your mother. Sixteen in a hospital bed with a newborn in your arms!!!!"

"I never be like that." Alani stormed out the kitchen.

Candice followed behind her. "Where you going?"

"For a walk." Alani opened the door and then slammed it shut as she walked out.

Feeling furious Candice screamed and sat on the couch. She took a deep breath and pulled out her blunt box. She rolled one and quickly lit it. She tried to relax but Austin came in and went straight upstairs. Candice followed him to her room and slammed the door behind her. He looked at her and sat up.

"Who pissed you off today?" Asked Austin.

"I don't know, you tell me." Candice answered angrily.

"I don't have time for your shit today."

"OH, you don't have time for my shit, but you have time for everything else."

Austin got up and walked up to Candice. He smiled as he touched her face. The he backhand her so hard she fell to the floor. She laid there and started to cry. Austin rolled his eyes and picked her up.

"I'm sorry babe." He said as he's hugging her and wiping her face. "You know can't talk to me like that. I don't take disrespect too kindly. How about I take you shopping, we go out to eat, and take a nice bubble bath with some champagne and slow jams. Have candles lit with you and me just chilling and good vibes. Would you like that?"

Candice thought about it. "Ok." She said smiling.

"There that smile. Get dress so we can go."

Candice ransacked all her drawers and closet. She rushed to the bathroom and jumped in the shower. Austin went downstairs and waited for Candice to get ready. He seen Candice blunt, lit it and smoke it.

He said to himself laughing. "Austin, you still got it."

Alani walked to Shadaya's house..........

She knocked on the door and Ms. Giles answered.

"Is Shadaya home?" Alani asked.

"Yeah sweety she home. SHADAYA, ALANI AT THE DOOR!!!"

Shadaya came running out the kitchen and grabbed Alani by the arm. They rushed upstairs to her room. Shadaya pulled out a box stashed away in her closet. She grabbed two plastic cups, and a bottle of 1800, a blunt and two cans of sprite out the box. She made some drinks and handed one to Alani. They both sat on her bed and Shadaya lit the blunt. Then she passed it to Alani who took a long puff.

"Let me tell you about the conversation we had about, after his conversation with his uncle. And you know what he told me."

"What?"

"That there is a gang in New York called Red Bandits. But he wasn't part of the group, his dad and Austin was."

"So, his uncle lied."

"Yeah, but that's not it. The reason they moved is because Austin screwed them out of money. So, they came after his dad because they couldn't find Austin."

"Damn that's crazy."

"I know, then he lied to Princeton saying that he shouldn't trust me because I'm sneaky."

"Why would he say that?"

"I don't know he's weird."

"Sooo, tell me about what you and Princeton got going on. I've seen you guys hugging and kissing. I put two and two together and it made sense."

"After our talk, we went to burger world and he walked me home. And when we got there, nobody was home. He hugged me and walk away but then he turned around and kissed me."

Shadaya got excited. "What happened next."

"We pretty much hung out in my room. All of sudden he asked me if I wanted to be his girlfriend."

"What you say?"

"I said yes."

Shadaya screamed and started to jump up and down clapping her hands. Alani signal her to calm down.

"You're going to be surprised after I tell you this."

"Tell me."

"Well while we kiss and cuddled, he told before he's a virgin. So, we both decided to be our first."

Shadaya fell back covering her smile and scream. She's happy for Alani and that she found someone for good.

"Well let me know when to buy my maid of honor dress."

"We are not getting married."

"What? Why not, ya'll moving faster than a speed train. I need to be prepared for when ya'll get engaged next month."

They both sat there and laughed.

"Oh, and one more thing. My Aunt Candice found out. So, now She wants to put me on birth control."

"Don't be mad, but I agree. I don't need my drinking partner being a teen mom. We got so much ahead of us and so much freedom. But it's your body. So, at the of the day you make the choice. Whatever happens I got your back for life. Even when were dead, I'll be knocking on your casket, like bitch let me tell you about this one time I visit this dude's grave…."

Alani laughed, but she felt grateful to have Shadaya for a friend. She has been there for Alani since they were kids. There was even a time when they were nine, Shadaya told Alani they can share her mom and live with them if she wanted to. Shadaya connected her phone to her Bluetooth speaker. Shadaya poured two shots in each cup and give Alani hers.

"Cheers, to your new relationship and losing your virginity. Your all grown up now." Said Shadaya with a fake cry.

When Ed Sheeran Shape Of You came on, they started to dance.

"I like to dedicate this song to you Alani."

"I hate you."

"I love you too."

They laughed and continued to dance. Alani felt better after the conversation she had with Candice. Alani phone let out a notification sound. They stopped and thought it was Candice trying to reach Alani. But when she checked her phone it was from Princeton.

I been thinking about you. I hope your day is going well. I love you.

Alani looked up at Shadaya who was staring the whole time with a nervous look on her face. She smiled and showed her the text message. The two got giddy and Alani text him back:

I love you too. Can't wait to see you tomorrow.

Then she got a call from Candice.

"Hello." She answered nervously.

"Hey Alani, I'm sorry I acted like that, but you my niece and I have to protect you cause I love you. Also, I got you scheduled for next week at the clinic. I think it best because I want you to enjoy your teenage years."

"I'm sorry too Aunt Candice. I will go to the clinic next week."

Alani hung up and threw her phone on the bed.

"Everything alright?" Shadaya asked.

"Yeah, I think everything going to be good for now on." She said with a smile. They hugged and finished dancing to the music on Pandora, drank some more and finished the blunt they started. All good things should happen for now on. Hopefully, it stay that way for Alani even after her Sixteenth birthday.

December 24, 2018

One day until Alani's 16th Birthday

Chapter 10

It's Christmas Eve in Tampa Bay, Florida. The sun is shining, and the weather is warm. Alani is one day away from her sixteenth birthday. Candice is finishing last bit of her surprise party with the help of Joey. Even though Joey is upset about Alani and Princeton's relationship. He had a talk with Princeton and approved of his intentions. As for Austin he's pissed about the relationship, but for now, he's can care less about it, but as always, he got something up his sleeve.

Alani woke up to the sound of someone knocking on her door. She got up and opened the door and there was Candice with a black dress.

"I need you to try this on." Demanded Candice.

"What this for?" Alani asked feeling confused.

"It for your birthday photo shoot. I have to have something to go with your cake."

"Ok."

Alani took the dress and tried it on. It fit nicely, It's open in the front with ruffles on the bottom attach underneath is shorts. The top is strapless with black sparkles all over the top and white diamond on the front and a white diamond belt around the waist.

"I love this dress. It so pretty and fit perfectly." Alani said looking in the closet door mirror.

"I glad you like it. Ok now give it back so it won't get dirty."

Alani took off the dress and gave it back to Candice.

"Oh shit, I almost forgot Shadaya wanted me to tell you that ya'll have a nail appointment today at 3. So, get dress it's 1:30."

Alani quickly went through every drawer and closet and put something together. She quickly took a shower and got dress by the time she was done, it is 2:20. She had an enough time to put her hair in a ponytail. She check her phone and got a text message from Shadaya saying she's pulling up. She also noticed she had another text message from Princeton.

Morning babe, just seeing if you're woke, if not I'll hear from you later. Love you.

Alani texted back: *Sorry, I just woke up and seen your text message. I'm about to get my nails done with Shadaya. I'll call you later. Love you too.*

She grabbed her keys, phone, and her mini bookbag with her wallet in it and ran downstairs and out the door. She seen Shadaya sitting outside in the same truck her dad let her borrow.

"Your dad in town again?"

"Yeah, but this time I got a sibling I'm not claiming."

"Rude."

"What you mean rude, I never cared for him, his bitch, and the new little bitch he calls his daughter. I can care less about them anyway."

"If you don't care, then why you driving his truck?"

"Because I'm trying to get him to put it in my name."

"Only you. Hey, you can tell him that he's the best father ever and you need a car to get places while your mom at work." Alani laughed.

"Uhh, Ewwww. No. That man does not deserve the praise he's looking for."

They arrived at the nail salon and checked in. They picked out some colors to match their outfits tomorrow. They got their pedicure done first. Alani got her toes painted black with silver glitter. While Shadaya got black also, but hers is a plain black. Next, they got their nails done. Alani choose to get her nails done with black tips, sliver glitter strip and diamonds on each tip. Shadaya got the same thing, but without the glitter, the diamonds, and the glitter strip. They thought it will be cute to be twins for her birthday.

After their nail appointment, they went to Poppi's Pizza to figure out what to do next. They decided on bringing the gang together. Shadaya texted Kelcie, while Alani texted Princeton. They choose to meet up at Dave and Busters. When everyone showed up at Dave and Busters, They all met in the front where you get the game cards. Everyone choose the eat and play. Alani and Princeton went to the over to the zombie game. Princeton swiped his card and him and Alani held the gun together. Shadaya, Kelcie, and Aaron smiled at each other when they walk past them, while Daisy stood by the dance game in disappointment. Shadaya notice Daisy's look and walked over to her.

"You still mad about them being together?" Shadaya asked.

"I don't like how every time we all get together, those two always run off together or they have to be around each other." Said Daisy with anger.

"Well it something you have to get use to. They love each other and I'm happy for Alani, your cousin seems like he's good for her. And how did you feel when you and Aaron hooked up when he supposed to be like the brother of the group, and he used to be our weed dealer."

"Aaron is not related to any of you so, it's different. She don't even text me anymore to hang. It's always her and Princeton like we ain't even friends anymore."

"Well Princeton lives you, plus she does text you Daisy you just never answer back, or you have Princeton text back with some excuse saying that your phone is broken."

"That's cause whenever we plan something, Princeton has to be included. Like sometimes, I wish I should have stopped the relationship."

"Either way, they still would have ended up together. Even if you approve or not. He's your cousin, not your brother. He can make his own choice." Then Shadaya walked away.

Daisy tried to have a good time, but she couldn't help seeing Alani and Princeton holding each other and kissing. It made her feel like she was losing a friend and felt left out. That the thing that made her angry. They ended their day of fun, with cashing in their game card. Alani cashed her in first and got a few things and nerf football for Princeton. While Princeton spent all of his on a huge teddy bear and shot glasses for Alani. Once everyone got their stuff, they all went outside and got in their rides. Jamie picked up Kelcie, while Aaron, Daisy and Princeton waited for Dana.

When Dana arrived, Daisy and Aaron hopping in the car, as Princeton and Alani said good-bye with hugs and kisses. Princeton got in the car and they drove away. Shadaya and Alani got in the truck and drove off. Shadaya pulled up to Candice's house and parked in the driveway. Austin's car wasn't there so Alani felt relieved, but there was a car there she recognized.

"Thank god I don't have to wake up with that perv waiting by my bedroom door tomorrow." Alani said staring out the car window.

"Yeah, he better not fuck up your birthday or he's going to have something coming his way." Shadaya said angrily.

"You a gun somewhere I don't know about." Alani laughed.

Shadaya laughed. "I wish, but I will get two for both of us."

Alani hugged Shadaya and got out the car.

"By the way I'm going to wake your ass up at 12." Shadaya shouted out the driver's window and pulled off.

Alani giggled and walk to the house. When she got in, she seen Candice and Mikey were sitting on the couch talking to each other and checking things off on a paper.

"Hey, Uncle Mikey." Said Alani giving him a hug. "What this?"

"Nothing for you see." He said waving her off.

"Oh, Alani why don't you go see your dad in the kitchen. He wanted to pick a day out for your driver's test." Said Candice.

"Ok." She said skipping to the kitchen.

"Whew, that almost got blown." Candice said shaking her head.

In the kitchen Joey is on the phone customizing a car for Alani's surprise.

"Hey dad, what you doing?"

"I was looking at some rentals for your driver's test. What do you think of this one?"

Alani looked at his phone and seen the car he wanted to show her. It is exactly like what she wanted.

"I love this. You think they would be able to let us buy it?"

"I don't know I'll ask and see."

"Thanks dad, your best." Alani hugged him.

"Your welcome."

Alani rushed up to her room and laid in her bed. She took a moment and started thinking about her birthday tomorrow.

"One day left." She said to herself.

She looked at the top lock on her door and jumped up to grab the screwdriver out her closet. She unscrewed the lock off her door and placed it in her nightstand. She pulled out a chef's knife, taser, and pepper spray out of her drawer and placed it under her pillow. As nighttime came around and it was time to sleep, Alani kept her

door unlocked and went to bed. She mumbled to herself "Now,

I'm ready for you, you sick bastard."

Chapter 11

Alani jumped up to the sound of someone banging on her door. She rushed to the door and opened to see Shadaya, Princeton, Daisy, Aaron and Kelcie by the door singing happy birthday. She stood there and smiled. She blew out the candle on the chocolate cupcake and let everyone in her room.

"So, what's the first thing you're going to do for your birthday?" Asked Kelcie.

"Get her hair done." Shadaya said putting her bag on the bed. Inside is hair products, flat iron, curlers, and jet black clip-ins. Also, inside is a make-up kit.

"I know I got the bottles for tonight. Cause we have to celebrate." Said Kelcie with excitement.

"Well me and Aaron should head and get ready and go grab something to smoke." Daisy and Aaron got up to walk out the room. "You coming Princeton?"

"Nah, ya'll can go without me I'll stay here for a bit."

"Ok." Daisy said rolling her eyes walking away.

"I should start getting ready too." Then Kelcie got up to leave too.

"I wonder why everybody getting dressed?" Alani wondered.

"The surprise is that we are going to take you out to eat. I was your Aunt idea." Princeton lied as him and Shadaya winked at each other.

"Oh ok, where we going then?"

"That we can't tell you." Said Shadaya straighten her hair and adding clip-ins.

Six o'clock comes around and Shadaya just finishing up getting ready. Alani is dressed up in her black dress, black open toe heels, diamond necklace and the diamond bracelet Princeton gave her. Her hair is in loose curls with a diamond head piece.

Candice comes in the room. "It time to go girls."

They both grabbed everything they needed and rushed out. Outside in a limo waiting for them. As they were on their way to where they were going, Shadaya did the last minute touches of Alani's makeup and blindfolded her. When they arrived, Candice got out first and rushed in she told everyone to hide. She walked out and helped Shadaya assist Alani to the entrance of the Ballroom Building Northside of Tampa Bay. They took a few more steps in and removed the blindfold.

"SURPRISE!!!!" Everyone shouted.

Alani was taken aback, and she was definitely surprise. She went around and gave everyone a hug. From family member to friends. Princeton walked up to her with something behind his back.

"You look really good tonight." He said looking at her up and down. He handed her bouquet of two dozen roses.

"Thank you. You look handsome." Alani said smiling and giggling.

The DJ started the music to get the party started. Everyone was mingling on the dance floor. Shadaya grabbed Alani and they went on the dance floor. As they were dancing, Princeton, Daisy, and Aaron joined in. Shadaya pass Alani over to Princeton and those two started dancing. Everyone was having a good time, drinking, and smoking outside.

When the time came to say happy birthday. Everyone gathered around by the stage. Candice wheeled out the three tier cake. It was all black with a sliver glitter ribbons on each tier. On the bottom said Happy Birthday Alani. The top had two number candles saying sixteen with sparklers. Everyone started singing happy birthday once the candles were lit. On stage is Candice, Austin, on the left Shadaya and Princeton on each side of Alani and Joey and Mikey on the right next to the DJ. Alani blew out her candles and looked at Austin who smiling behind Candice. Alani smiling back at him. Little did he know she has been making plans to fight off Austin.

Mikey handed Joey the mic and walked off the stage. Everybody stood and watch what he had to say.

"I need everyone to head outside have another surprise for my little girl."

Once everyone was outside, Joey put his arm around Alani shoulder.

"I know you wanted that car, but I couldn't rent it because someone already brought it." Said Joey.

Alani looked at him in sadness until Mikey pulled up in an all-black 2018 Mercedes-Benz GLE-Class SUV wrapped in a red bow. Alani screamed and jumped up.

"You brought it. Thank you, dad." She hugged him with excitement and ran to the car. She got in and looked around everything about it she loved. She was so happy; it made her cry.

"Are you crazy to get that girl that type of car. She doesn't even have her permit yet." Candice said in anger.

"I can get her whatever she wants. She my daughter, and I want what's best for her."

"If Katrina was alive, she wouldn't be happy about this."

"Yeah, she wouldn't have been happy. But after seeing Alani's face she wouldn't care. If you remember, I been there for Alani since she was born."

"You know what, what if she wasn't your daughter. I bet you would think different."

Joey looked at her dead in the eye. "It wouldn't change shit."

Candice stomped away and into the building. Austin followed behind her.

"What up with you?" Austin asked.

"He could have to talk to me about getting Alani a car. This the shit I hate. He never wants to talk to me first about anything. How did he even get the money to afford the car? Then he throws it in my face mentioning that he's Alani's father. Like I'm not the one who took her in, feed her, and makes sure she straight. If he wanted to take care of Alani himself, why ain't she staying with him, why ain't he waking up early to take her to school. This pop up and buying her expensive shit is annoying and it pissing me off. He not even my baby daddy and he got me upset."

Austin tried to catch on to everything Candice was saying. (*How did Joey have the money to buy everything for the party and buy a car?*) He thought about it. Then a lightbulb went off. The only way he will know is if he makes Candice be the weasel and watch all of Joey's moves. But he would have to convince her to be friendly with Joey or make friends with Mikey and get him to talk. He walked over to Candice who was sitting at the table by the door. He whispered in her ear about his plan and Candice looked at him in disgust.

"Hey, we both want to know where the money come from and what moves he making to get it. Plus, he still owe me for the stash we were supposed to agree on." Said Austin trying to convincing her.

"What stash you talk about?" Candice asked confused.

"The one your sister died over. He told me that the deal is back on the table and this time he's coming through with it." Austin lied.

"No, me and Alani is not going to die because he fucked up again."

"Ya'll won't die because I need you on the inside. Plus, I won't hurt Alani. She's the reason he's still around. So, are you in? I'll pay you double plus extra."

Candice thought about it for second and then she said yes, she'll do it. Everyone back in after spending 20 minutes admiring Alani's new car. They finished party then slowly the crowd got smaller as people left to go home.

By 10:30pm, the cleaning crew came in and started to clean Austin and Candice got in Austin's car after she told the limo driver, he was good to end his shift. Kelcie, Daisy, and Aaron rode with Jamie to his house. Joey and Mikey hugged Alani good-bye and told her to be safe and enjoy her new car. Lastly, Alani got in the driver's seat with Shadaya in the front seat and Princeton in the back.

"Guys I need you to stay with me tonight." Said Alani as she try to focus on the road.

"I was going stay anyway." Said Shadaya taking off her heels.

"I will stay if you need me to." Said Princeton. "Why, what up?"

Alani took a deep breath. "Back when I was nine, Austin came in my room. He told me when I turned sixteen, he will turn me into a woman and make me his bitch."

"WHAT!!! WHO WOULD SAY THAT TO A NINE YEAR OLD. Sorry Princeton, but you uncle got problems."

"I wouldn't thought he be that type of person to go that far."

When they arrived, Austin car was in the driveway. Alani parked and they all got out. They walked in the house and went straight to Alani's room. Princeton closed the door and sat on the bed with Alani while, Shadaya sat in the furry beanie chair. Alani pulled out the knife, taser and pepper spray from underneath her pillow and placed them back in her drawer.

"What hell you have all that stuff?" Shadaya asked.

"I was preparing for him to break into room last night." Alani answer putting her stuff in the drawer.

After all, three got ready for bed, Shadaya slept on the pull out bed while Alani and Princeton slept in her bed. The clock hit 2:00am, The door creek open. He stood disappointed to see his nephew and Shadaya in Alani's room. He closed the door quietly and went downstairs. He lit a blunt and lay down on the couch and closed his eyes. Then he opened eye to find a gun pointed at his head.

"If you do anything to hurt Alani, won't hesitated to kill you." Princeton warned Austin.

Chapter 12

It's the day after the party and Alani wakes up with Princeton staring at his phone scrolling through Facebook. He has a tired look on his face. Ever since he left a warning to Austin. He turned to look at Alani who is staring at him smiling.

"Good morning babe." Princeton said smiling.

"Good morning to you too babe." Alani said leaning over to kiss Princeton. "You look like you haven't slept."

"Yeah, I haven't I been watching out for my uncle. I kinda left him a warning last night."

"Why would you do that?" Alani asked wandering.

"To let him know I got your back."

Alani smiled and they started kissing again.

"Hey if you guys are going be fucking, let me know when to leave the room." Said Shadaya looking over.

Alani and Princeton laughed. He got up and walked out the room to use the bathroom.

After he was done, he walked out and suddenly he felt someone snatch him up and carry him downstairs with his mouth covered by someone's hand. Fighting to get away, they threw him in the trunk and put a bag over his head. They tied him up and closed the trunk. Princeton felt every turn and the car stopping and going. The car took one final turn and then it suddenly stopped. Princeton can feel someone yank him out the trunk. They dragged him inside a house and sat him on the couch. They took the bag off and Princeton seen Austin and Devin standing in front of him.

"You thought I was going to let you slide with that little threat you made last night." Austin said laughing. "You're lucky, your family or you wouldn't have woken up today. I'm happy that your dad allow me to give you a warning."

He signaled Devin to walk over to Princeton. He stood over him punched straight in the eye. Then he started beating him until Austin stopped him once the blood leaked out mouth. Princeton rolled over and tried to catch his breath.

"Now you know next time, don't threaten me. Especially, over a bitch you just met. Take him back and leave him in the living room. And if they see you don't explain shit. Just say you found him."

Jaime nodded his head and gripped up Princeton and carried him to the car. Once they got back to Candice's house, Jamie carried Princeton into the house and dropped him in the living room floor. He rushed back out, jumped in the car, and sped off. Alani came out the kitchen and seen Princeton struggling to get on the couch. She screamed and ran over to him with Shadaya behind her.

"Princeton you ok? What happened to you?" Alani asked in a panic.

"I think Austin didn't take my warning lightly." Said Princeton hunching over in pain.

Shadaya took Princeton to the kitchen to clean him off. She told Alani to go upstairs to her room because she can the fear in her eyes, as tears rolled down cheeks. She went back in the kitchen and grabbed a towel to clean him off. She wiped his face and made an ice bag for him.

"This is why nobody fucks with your uncle. He will do some shady shit."

"I thought he will back off a little."

"Prince, he's Austin, he don't care if you kiss the ground he walks on, he will still step on head."

Alani came back down and into the kitchen. She rushed over and hugged Princeton.

"Oww, babe that hurts." Said Princeton in pain.

"I'm sorry." Alani apologized with concern. "Why would he do this to you? You're his nephew."

"I realized he doesn't care. He only cares about himself and reputation. Alani, I think you should tell your dad. If he would do this to me who knows what he do to you if we're not around."

"I can't, I don't want to make things worse than what it is."

"I'm sorry Alani, but he's right you need to tell him and your aunt too."

"Ok I'll try, but I feel like shit is going to go downhill. I can see if my dad wants to meet me tomorrow."

In Joey's house.........

Joey and Mikey sat at the round table downstairs in the finished basement. They are discussing new products and new moves with their new crew members Charlie (Mikey's nephew), Byron, and Felix (former crew members of Austin's).

"Aight, somehow Austin put the deal back on the table with the vape oil we were supposed to sell. So, we have to come up some new products that he won't be able to touch or know about." Said Joey calmly.

"My brother got this new batch of Rainbow Haze. He's looking for people to buy from him." Felix offered.

"What does it do?" Asked Mikey.

"It makes you zone out and you start seeing shit in different colors."

Joey looked at Mikey who didn't look too interested in what Felix was trying to convince him to buy.

"We'll keep that in mind. Anything else?" Mikey quickly moved on to the next idea.

"I know Austin trying something new. I heard it supposed to be good." Said Byron.

"We trying to cut ties from Austin, not get into more shit with him." Said Mikey

"If we can have someone on the outside that cool with Austin or his people, then they can watch their movements and get back to us with the hot spots and what he's up to next, so we'll be ahead of the game." Said Byron laying out a plan.

"This is Austin you're talking about. If he find out what we all are up to, we ain't going be seeing the next day." Mikey warned.

"I can do it. Aaron my bro. Sometimes he's in on every move Austin make. Plus, I can have Princeton give me some insight since he's with Alani."

"No, leave Princeton out of it. I don't need Alani in some shit because of him." Said Joey getting upset.

Joey phone let out a loud notification noise. He went to look at it and got a text message from Alani.

Hey dad, you think you got time tomorrow to talk. It something I really need to tell you.

Joey heart dropped to his stomach whatever it is he hoped she's not becoming a teenage mom.

Joey texted back: *yeah, I got plenty of time. You need me to come over?*

No, I can drive there, will Mikey be there too? I'm going to need both of you to hear this.

No, but I'll let him know.

Ok. I'll ya'll tomorrow.

"What's that about?" Asked Mikey.

"It's Alani, She says she has something to tell us tomorrow."

"She want to talk to you and me?"

"Yeah."

"It must be something serious. I hope it don't have to do anything Austin. He got us back in this deal again, I don't want to fuck this up again."

They continue their meeting and agreed to hold off on the coming up with the product and find what popular in the streets first. Charlie is good at knowing what's popular with the teens, while Byron and Felix find what the adults like.

Everyone got dismissed and went home. Joey sat at the table and put his head on his hands. He took a moment to himself.

"You ok bro?" Asked Mikey.

"Yeah, I just need a minute."

"Ok, I'll you tomorrow, hopefully it's something good."

"Yeah, or shits going to get bad real fast."

Chapter 13

Joey woke up the next day with a knot in his stomach. He got up and jump in the shower. He let the water run down on his head as he leaned against the shower wall. Twenty minutes later, he got out and threw on a white tee shirt, grey sweatpants, and white socks. Then wrapped a towel around his locs to dry them off. He sat on the living room couch, rolled a blunt and lit it. Joey turned on the tv and changed the channel to ESPN. He sat there and smoked hoping it will make him feel better. Joey got up and looked out the window. He seen a red 2013 Chevrolet Malibu pulled up to the side of the house.

Then he sat back on the couch and continue to watch tv. Next thing he heard the door closed and someone walking upstairs.

"What up bro, you look a little relaxed." Mikey joked.

"I wish, Alani got me nervous. I don't know I something happened to her, if she's pregnant, or something that Candice did or Austin."

"It'll be fine bro, she knows better and if it about Austin or Candice, we'll handle it. Let's calm down and hope it's good news."

Suddenly the alarm went off. Joey and Mikey jumped and pulled their guns.

"DAAAD!!!! YOU UPSTAIRS?!" Yelled Alani.

"YEAH, UP HERE!!!" Joey yelled back.

He disabled the alarm from his phone, and both put their guns away. Alani came upstairs with Princeton behind her. They both sat on the couch and Princeton kept his head down.

"Who is this?" Asked Joey.

"It's Princeton." Alani answered.

Princeton took off the hood of his hoodie and glasses.

"What hell happen to you?" Asked Mikey concerned.

"Well it's something that I was scared to tell you."

"Did he hurt you?" Joey got worried.

"No dad, he was protecting me. From Austin."

"What the fuck did Austin do?"

"Well back when I was nine, he came into my room and told me after my sixteenth birthday he will make me a woman and turn me into his bitch."

"I threaten him, and he took me to Devin's house and had Devin beat me." Princeton explained.

"Why the hell would you do that. You should know your uncle." Said Mikey.

"Yeah, I know now. I never really knew much about him. He left my dad's house when I was two. I just wanted to give him a warning not to hurt her."

Joey stood there starting at Princeton's swollen face. Just hearing him say he was protecting Alani and seeing his beaten face shows him that he really cares for her. It also made him feel bad Princeton. Then hearing about what Austin why going to do to Alani made him angry. Then lightbulb went off in Mikey's head.

"Bro, I know you don't want to hear this, but I think Austin is using Alani to seal the deal for good." Said Mikey.

Then Joey thought about it. If the deal doesn't fall through, then Austin will keep Alani to himself until it does. Alani sat watched Joey pace back and forth. She didn't know what was going through his head, but she thinks it's not good.

"What should we do?" Asked Mikey.

"We're going to have a talk with Candice."

Joey and Mikey jumped in Mikey's car, while Alani and Princeton jumped in hers. They drove back to Candice house and when they got there, they jumped out and walked in. Feeling furious Joey barged in, with Mikey behind him. They both kept a gun on them seeing that Austin's car in the driveway also. He rushed upstairs and banged on Candice's bedroom door until she answered it.

"Why the hell you banging on my door like you're the cops?" Candice asked angrily.

"I need to talk to you." Said Joey

"About?"

"Your niece."

"Give me a minute, I'll be downstairs." She slammed door closed.

Joey, Mikey, Alani, and Princeton sat in the living room and waited. Candice came downstairs, grabbed a chair from the kitchen and sat down.

"Where's Austin?" Asked Mikey.

"He's upstairs, why you want him to come down too?"

"No this is family business."

"What's going on Alani?" Candice asked.

Alani took a deep breath. "Austin told me when I was nine that after my sixteenth birthday, he was going to make me his bitch."

Candice look at Alani like she was lying. "Why would you make something like that up?"

They all look at Candice like she was crazy.

"ARE YOU FUCKING STUPID!!! You don't see the shit he does Candice." Joey yelled in anger. "He had someone beat up his own nephew because he wanted to protect Alani."

"Well told me Princeton put a gun to his head and started being disrespectful."

"That cause he protecting you niece. Come on Candice you really going to believe that bullshit?"

"Well ya'll get the fuck out. I don't have time for your shit."

"Alani, go pack your stuff." Joey demanded.

Alani went straight upstairs and into her room.

"Joey this bullshit, you not just going to come here and take Alani away from me."

"I'm her father and I have a right to."

"Don't pull that I'm her father bullshit with me. Where were you to pick up Alani after Katrina died huh? I had to wake up early and take her to school, feed her, made sure she's straight for the rest of her life. I took care of her like she was my own. Here you come popping up whenever you wanted to see her."

"I was trying to get my shit together for her. I didn't want her staying with me because I was fuck up in the head after finding out that Katrina died. I need to stack up so that I can have enough for her to live a good life. Don't think I didn't care because I been there for her every day. You forgot I got shot too. I had to hide out cause the person your messing with wanted me dead. I thank god every day that I got to live to see Alani grow up. She wasn't only Katrina world, she mine too."

Alani came back down with bags filled with her stuff. Candice grabbed one of her bags begging her to stay, but Mikey ripped her hand away and Joey walked out with her with Princeton behind her. Candice cried and fell to the floor. Austin came downstairs and stood over her. He shook his head and then tapped his foot on her head. She looked up and saw him looking at her in disappointment.

"You could have just gone along with it. Would have made them be on your side, but nope you want to be a bitch and ruin everything for me. Now I might not have a done deal with those two. So now, your ass going to starve."

He walked out and left. Candice cried even more knowing that she barely any money to live off for the next two months.

The group went back to Joey's house after Princeton packed his stuff too. Alani asked Joey if it was ok for Princeton to stay with them. At first, he didn't like the idea. But since he took a beating trying to scare off Austin, he figured it would hurt. But it pissed off Daisy because now she felt like Alani was taking away her only family member her age that she can talk to and hang with.

Joey had them placed in separate rooms because he didn't want anything going on that he don't know about under his roof. Nighttime comes and Joey ordered some food from Grubhub. He got four burgers, two large fries, three drinks and a chocolate shake for Alani. They were all relaxing, until Alani got a text from Daisy.

It says: *You're going to pay bitch, what has my father done to you for you to be spreading lies? Then you're going to have my cousin turn against him. I hope whatever comes your way, puts you in the same place where your mother sleeping.*

Alani forward Princeton the text. He looked at the message and texted Alani back: *Don't worry she just pissed off right now, But if it really a problem me and Shadaya will handle it.*

Alani read the text and smiled. She tapped Princeton on his side, and he look at her. She mouthed I love you and he smiled and mouthed I love you too. Then they went back to watching the movie. When it was over, Mikey left and went home. Joey went his room and stayed there for a few hours. Around that time, Alani and Princeton are in her room cuddling. An hour later, Joey knocked on the door and opened it and seen the two laughing.

"Hey, separate, it time for bed." Joey demanded and went back to his room.

"I guess I'll see you in the morning." Said Princeton smiling.

"Yeah." Said Alani making a sad face.

They kissed each other good night and he headed off to the guest room across the hall. Alani laid in bed and stared at the ceiling until she fell asleep.

In Joey's room, seeing the way Alani and Princeton giggled at each other made him think about him and Katrina when they were sixteen. He went through the drawer in his nightstand and pulled out an old picture of him and Katrina at the photo booth in the mall. Katrina had her hair in a bun and wore minimal makeup with hoop earrings and Joey locs reach passed his ears and over his eyes. He had on diamond earrings and wore a short chain necklace with Katrina's

159

name on it hanging off of it. They were hugging as Joey kissed her on the cheek and she was smiling. It hurt just to look at this picture because she wasn't here to laugh with him about that day. He put back in the drawer and he turned down the volume on the tv to listen to the noise outside his room. He closed his eyes and silently cry himself to sleep.

Chapter 14

Joey woke up to the sun shining in his face. Rising up from his bed, he opened his crust-filled eyes from tears he cried last night. He walked to the kitchen to make him something to eat. In the kitchen Alani was attempting to make breakfast while Princeton sat and watched her in admiration.

"HEY!!!" Joey said slapping Princeton on the back of his head. "Keep staring at her like that, you won't have no eyes to look."

"Sorry." Said Princeton looking away.

"I could made breakfast if you were hungry." Joey sat down and pulled out a duffle bag from under the table.

"It's ok dad, you've done enough for us."

Joey waved Alani off form the stove and finished off the food. He made plates for all three of them. As they sat and ate Joey laid out the ground rules.

"First off ground rules around here. Rule number one, no sleeping in the same beds. Two, no company unless I'm in the house or I know them. Three, don't touch anything here unless asked. Four, don't answer the door, if you know who it is, it's fine if not, ignore it. Unless I tell you, who coming. Can ya'll follow the rules?"

"Yes." They both said.

As they started eating Princeton asked a question.

"Joey, can I ask you something personal?"

"Yeah."

"What were you and Alani's mom like?"

Joey looked up from the blunt he started to roll and stared at the wall. All those feelings he felt before and after Katrina died, came back. He tried his hardest not to cry. Alani looked at Joey,

he looked back at her, smile, and gave her a few taps on her hand. Letting her know he was ok to talk about it.

"We were good……. Shit everything was good. We did a lot of stupid shit. We used to steal her parents car and go places just to chill, and talk. Back when me and your uncle were bros. We all just do random shit out of boredom. We all were one big crew until Katrina got pregnant with Alani. Then we fell out because Austin was telling Devin that Katrina was up to something and he couldn't trust her. I defended for her cause I know Katrina wouldn't do that. Plus, she dump Devin cause he was cheating on her and he got upset when she ended up with me. So, Austin cut us off cause I broke the rule of the guy code. Never date your bro's ex. I didn't give a shit. I loved Katrina and Austin started to get real sneaky with shit. I kept my distance until I needed the money for Katrina and Alani."

"What happened to her?"

Joey took a deep breath and clenched his fist.

"It all started with this deal I had with uncle. I missed out on the meeting, so he sent out people to look for me. They shot me then they ended up shooting her. I don't why, but people said she died on scene and Alani was placed in some shelter until her Aunt Candice pick her up."

"How long were you in the hospital?"

"Almost a month. They said I'm lucky the bullets didn't hit anything major. Everything was my fault, I forgot I had meet up with him. I just wanted to spend time with Katrina and Alani. I didn't get that much time cause I was so busy coming up with something new for your uncle to sell."

"He could have cut you some slack. Knowing you were with Alani. He should know about fatherhood."

"Wow, you seriously don't know your uncle. Austin is a self-centered asshole. He only cares when it's about him."

"Yeah, I'm starting to know now that I should keep my distance from him."

"You should, not to make you go against your uncle, but to stay out of his shit."

"Yeah, I think I'm going have to cut family ties just to avoid him."

"You sure you want to do that babe?" Asked Alani with concern.

"Yeah, Daisy not going to talk to me from what she posted. My parents I assume their upset because they feel like I traded on my uncle for you, and that I left. It sucks, but I don't want to be in any bad blood between Joey and Austin."

"At least your uncle won't be able to turn you into a manipulative asshole. Cause you got us." Said Alani giving him a hug and kiss.

"Alani." Said Joey in a stern voice.

"What? Is it because I kiss him."

"No, your mouth."

"Oh, sorry dad."

Alani got a text from Shadaya. It said: *Call me, now!!!*

Alani rushed to her room as she called Shadaya and the boys continue the conversation.

"Hey, what's wrong?" Alani asked concerned.

"Check your Facebook. Daisy wrote some bullshit on her page about you and Princeton."

Alani went to look on Daisy's Facebook page, but she got blocked.

"She blocked me." Alani became upset.

"She block you too. Oh, now she really want her ass beat." Shadaya said angrily.

"What she say?" Alani asked interested.

"She said: {It's crazy how someone closes to will have your own blood turn on you. All because of a lie. Once shit like that happens, it time to cut them off. Years don't matter when they show their true colors.} Then I comment saying: {If your bold enough to say that, then be direct.}

"I've done nothing to her, nothing. And she's mad because of what her father told me. Oh, I forgot, she's a spoiled daddy's girl that sees nothing wrong for what he does. At least Princeton knows what kind of uncle he is. He's talking about cutting them all off."

"Really?"

"Yeah, he said he don't want to be in any bad blood between Austin and my dad."

"He needs to, he's better off being with you guys. He family seem like their snakes and delusional."

"I guess we won't be seeing Daisy anymore."

"I hope not. If I ever see that bitch again, she's getting dropped."

"Yeah, I got some words for her. You doing anything tomorrow?"

"No, why?"

"Nothing much, I don't have anything planned."

"I guess we're going to Hotspot then."

"See that why I always depend on you when it comes to planning."

"Yup, I'll see you tomorrow."

Alani went back into the kitchen and seen the guys were gone. So, she checked the living room and the guys are sitting on the couch watching a football game. The two talking about what team has the chance to make it to the Super Bowl after this game.

He looks at his phone to check for messages and he got one from Candice. It said: *I need to talk to you when you have the time. Can you tell Alani that I miss her, and I love her.*

Joey texted back: *Ok, but I'm bringing Mikey with me in case you want to pull some bullshit.*

She said: *I promise you, I won't set you up.*

Joey put his phone back ion the nightstand and went to sleep.

Chapter 15

Joey got up and got ready to meet Candice. He took his shower, then ate a bowl of cereal and checked both rooms. He went into the living room and seen Alani and Princeton cuddled up on the couch.

"I'm heading out to meet your aunt. Ya'll remember the rules right"

"Yeah dad, we're going to be leaving later anyway."

"Where you going?"

"Hotspot."

"Ok, text me when you leave."

"Ok."

Joey walked out and got in his car. He drove to Candice house texting Mikey to see if he's there. Once he pulled up to

Candice's house, Mikey was sitting in his car waiting. They both got out and walked in Candice house. She was laying on the couch naked, drinking Jack Daniels out the bottle.

"Can you at least put some clothes on when you people over." Said Joey looking away.

Candice rolled her eyes and wrapped the cover around her.

"So, what is so important that you needed to tell me?"

"What's sup motherfuckers. What going on with that deal we were supposed to sign off on…...TWO MONTHS AGO!!!" Said Austin upset.

"Look man just give us some time. We been trying to get shit together……."

"I gave enough time." Austin interrupted. "I been wanting this shit six years ago and I still don't have it. I want it now or I will be the last person you'll see before I put you two fuckers to sleep."

Joey looked at Candice who gave him the 'well' shrug.

"Alright, we'll get it to you today." Said Mikey.

"Good, and to make sure you get it, Joey is going to stay here with me. And if don't have it by the end of today. You going to be the last crew member standing."

Mikey got up and walked out the door. Austin tapped Candice with the gun and gave it her. He told her to stand by Joey and watch him while he head off to the kitchen. Candice did exactly what she was told.

"Candice, I thought I told you no bullshit." Said Joey.

"We all need the money."

"Is it for the money or to keep Austin around?"

"Hmm, both."

As they waited for Mikey to come back, later in the day.......

Alani and Princeton got ready to go out with Shadaya to Hotspot.
When they were ready to go, Alani texted Shadaya to see if she's
ready. She got a text back saying she's ready. They grabbed
everything they need, got in the car, and drove to Shadaya's. Once
they picked her up, they are their way to Hotspot. When they got there,
they drove around in circles. Saturday nights are the most crowded.
They found one parking spot, after the person that was parked there
left.

They walked in and the place didn't seem that crowded on the
teen side. On the adults side, it was party. You can silhouette of people
shoulder to shoulder. All three sat down at the tables by the snack bar.
They were deciding on what they should do first. They did go-carting

first then bowling next. When they got done with go-carting they went over to the bowling alley.

They sat down at the bowling tables and seen Daisy, Aaron, Kelcie and Gia sitting three tables across from them. Alani turned around in her seat and Shadaya looked away in disgust.

"I see someone getting friendly with the side chick, cause she don't got no real friends."

Princeton waved as Aaron got a glimpse of them. Aaron waved back, got up and walked over to them.

"WHAT'S UP BRO!!!" Aaron shouted and smacked him on the back.

"Hey man." Princeton said smiling.

"We ain't got no problems between us. Right?"

"We cool, nothing changed."

"Since when did Gia and Daisy get along?" Asked Alani.

"I don't know, but that shit weird. It's making me uncomfortable. Makes me think she's up to something." Said Aaron getting suspicious.

"She probably is. Just watch your back." Shadaya warned.

"BABE!!!" Daisy shouted.

"Yeah, I'ma go back over there I think she's getting pissed."

"Fuck that bitch." Said Shadaya giving the finger over Daisy's way.

Daisy jumped up, but Kelcie pulled back down.

"It not worth it Daisy, she's Shadaya." Said Kelcie.

"No, IF SHE GOT A PROMBLEM, WE CAN HANDLE IT RIGHT NOW!!!!" Daisy shouted.

"Shadaya she's just testing you." Said Alani trying to keep her calm.

177

"Well, bitch I failed." Shadaya said jumping up. "DAISY, GET YOUR SCARY ASS UP AND FIGHT ME!!!"

Daisy jumped up again tried to rush over to Shadaya, but Kelcie held her back.

"LET HER GO KELCIE, SHE CAN TALK SHIT ON FACEBOOK AND BLOCK PEOPLE, SHE CAN THROW HANDS."

Kelcie let go of Daisy and Shadaya pulled her hair up into a ponytail. Daisy ran up to Shadaya and threw the first punch. Then Shadaya start swinging back hitting Daisy a couple of times. Then they both hit the ground, with Shadaya on top of her throwing punches. A whole crowd of teens ran over to watch the fight. Even a few adults watched the fight. Alani pulled Shadaya off and Kelcie grabbed Daisy. They all went outside then Daisy ran up and grabbed Shadaya hair and threw punches.

"Let go of my hair bitch." Shadaya said angrily.

Shadaya grabbed Daisy's hair and then Kelcie went over and started pulling Shadaya's hands off of Daisy's hair. Shadaya wouldn't let go, so Kelcie started punching Shadaya in the head. Then those two started fighting. Daisy looked over at Alani. Alani pushed Princeton back and both charged at each other throwing punches. Princeton ran over and grabbed Alani. Daisy got up, ran over to Aaron, and pulled a gun out his pocket. She aimed at Alani and fired a shot. Princeton quickly grabbed Alani and used himself as a shield. Princeton collapsed on top of Alani. Aaron went to grab the gun from Daisy, but as he struggled to get it away from her, more shots rang out.

People ran away screaming, Princeton rolled over and got up in pain. He helped Alani up and she started to panic from seeing the blood drip down his right shoulder on his back. Quickly, Alani, Shadaya, and Princeton jumped in Alani's car. Shadaya ended up driving while Alani kept the wound patched up with her jacket. She held on to Princeton and started to cry.

"I'll be fine babe." He said as he held on to Alani.

As Mikey came back with the stash of vape oil.......

Joey and Mikey gave Austin the vape oil. They actually felt relieved it was done, but upset they couldn't fall through with their plan. Austin phone started to ring.

"I'm getting shit wrapped up with this deal right now, what's up?"

"Austin, we need to meet up at your crib now. Somebody was shooting and Daisy said it was her."

"WHO THE FUCK WAS SHE SHOOTING AT?" Austin yelled.

"I don't know, she won't say. She in the back of car trippin' saying she gonna kill em'."

"Ok, I'm leaving now."

Austin hung up shaking his head.

"What happened?" Candice asked.

Austin didn't answer and rushed out the door.

"Who was shooting?" Mikey wondered.

Joey looked at his phone. He had a missed called from Alani. He called her back.

"Hey, you home?"

"No, I'm at the hospital."

Joey got worried. "Why are you at the hospital?"

"Princeton got shot."

"How the hell that happened?"

Alani hesitated to answer.

"Alani?!"

"I'll explain it to you when you get here." Then she hung up.

"What happened?" Mikey asked

"Alani at the hospital, she said Princeton got shot." Joey said jumping and walking out the door. Mikey followed behind him, while Candice stayed.

Chapter 16

It's the next day and Joey is up cleaning and re-patching Princeton's wound. Princeton is wincing in pain.

"I been shot before, I know how painful it is, the shit sucks." Said Joey putting a fresh patch on his wound.

"Is Alani ok, she been crying all night?" Asked Princeton.

"Yeah she's fine. She just got scared from what happened."

"Thanks for helping me out."

"Your welcome." Joey patted him on the shoulder.

Princeton went into Alani's room. In there. she was still sleep in her bed from crying all night. Princeton went back to his room and waited until she woke up. An hour later, he felt a tap on his shoulder. He turned to see who it is.

"You ok?" Princeton asked.

"Yeah, sorry if I freak out last night, I got scared. It just that seeing you shot, reminded me of that night my mom died."

"Yeah, I seen the fear in your eyes, that's why I been so calm."

Alani phone started to ringing in her room. She rushed over to answer it.

"Hello." Alani answered.

"Hey girl, how you feeling?" Asked Shadaya.

"I'm alright, that night shouldn't have went left."

"At least she got a taste of what I wanted to give her. I hope it shut her up. But I know she's on Facebook talking shit. Anyways, how Princeton doing?"

"He good, my dad been helping him clean his stitches."

"Awe, he such a good father-in-law." Shadaya laughed.

Alani laughed. "Yeah, we'll see in the next five years."

"You mean in two months."

"Don't push it." Alani laughed.

Back at Austin's house.......

Daisy is still upset about what happened last night. She was laying in the bed, scrolling through her Facebook. Every post on her timeline talks about last night. Some even posted the fight before the shooting. Her door cracked open and Austin walked in.

"We need to talk about the dumb shit you did last night." Austin sat down on her bed.

Daisy put down her phone and sat up on her bed.

"I'm sorry dad, I just got mad because Shadaya kept messing with me. Then seeing Alani just made it even worse. All could think about is that lie she said about you."

"Let her lie. If you don't believe it, then it's not true to you princess."

"Dad I'm 17, you can stop calling me princess."

"But you're still my little girl. One question, where did you get a gun from?"

"Aaron."

"Well I'm going to have a talk with Aaron about that. Other than that, don't worry about Alani. Killing her ain't going to make things better unless you get rid of the people around her. Just remember keep…."
"Your friends close, but your enemies closer, I remember dad." Daisy interrupted.

"Ok. You don't have to be friends with her, but keep an eye out and just on her, your cousin too."

Austin got up and walked out her room. She didn't care about the keeping enemies close, she just wanted to ruin them for revenge. They something came to mind. She went on Facebook and created a fake page with the name Rebecca. She looked through google and pick out some pictures. After she created the page, she added everyone on her friend list including Alani family and Shadaya's. She claimed that she is old friend that Alani and Shadaya forgot about.

She started to post secrets to the timeline. The first one was about Alani and Princeton losing their virginity to each other. Then Shadaya having sex in the school bathroom during lunch. Then she said Princeton used to skipped school to sell weed. Next, she started with the rumors. Shadaya had two pregnancy scares and one abortion. Alani and Princeton are planning to elope after finding out she's pregnant. The she posted saying that Shadaya is a sugar baby. She sat back and watched all of the comments flow in. The reactions were from shocked to angry. Daisy smiled, knowing this will start to cause drama between Alani, Princeton, and Shadaya.

Back at Joey's house......

Candice gave texted Joey telling him what was posted on Facebook. He went to Daisy's fake page Rebecca to see it for himself. In anger, he jumped up and rushed to Princeton's room and gripped him up and walked to Alani room holding on to his shirt. He kicked in Alani door making her jump out of her sleep.

"LIVING ROOM, NOW!!!" He yelled.

Alani got up, slowly walked out her room and into the living room. She can see the fear in Princeton face telling her something is not good. She sat down on the couch next to him. Then Joey came out the kitchen with a chair and sat down.

"Do either of you want to tell me what the fuck is going on."

"What's going on?" Asked Alani

"Don't pretend to be stupid, I already know. I just need to confirm it."

"Confirm what dad?"

"Your aunt told some stuff she seen on your old friend's Facebook saying that you're pregnant and planning to elope."

"WHAT, what friend you're talking about?"

"Her name Rebecca."

"I don't know who that is."

"Well she knows you. You don't remember her from somewhere?"

"No, I never met somebody name Rebecca. All those things your reading is not true. Princeton you know anybody named Rebecca?"

"No."

"For now on, Princeton your going have to go back to Austin's until Alani come back from the clinic."

"WHAT!!!! That's not fair. I told you is not true."

"That's how it's going to go for now. I'll find out the truth once I get the results. Princeton start packing."

"DAD!!!" Alani yelled.

"I don't care, I can't have my 16 year old daughter pregnant just because she want to live a fucking fairytale life."

Alani got up, walked to her room, and slammed the door. Princeton got up and went to his room to start packing. When he was done, he went to Alani's room to say good-bye. He gave her a hug and kiss and told her it will be alright, he'll be back.

Princeton and Joey got in the car. Joey drove to Austin's house.

"It's only for one day. I'm not let you stay with somebody you don't trust for good." Said Joey in a nice way.

He pulled up to Austin's house and parked. Princeton stared at Austin's house, he could feel his stomach turn and his heart drop. He opened the car door and stood there.

"Don't make it any harder than what it is. If Austin does anything to you, you let me know. I'll pick you up tomorrow after Alani's visit at the clinic."

"Ok." He closed the door and walking towards the house. Him And Joey waved to each other and Princeton closed the front door.

Inside the tv is on and he could hear someone in the kitchen.

"MOM!!! IS THAT YOU?" Princeton shouted.

Dana came running out the kitchen.

"MY BABY!!!" Dana screamed. She gave Princeton a hug and gave him a bunch of kisses on his cheek.

"Hey mom." Said Princeton smiling.

"How you feeling?"

"I'm good, for now."

"What makes you say that?"

"The situation that happened with Daisy."

"Ooohh, yeah. Well we won't be staying here for long. Your father brought us a house northside of Tampa."

"Will Austin be there visiting?"

"Not likely. You know your father don't be home most of the time because he always on the move."

Princeton was happy that he don't get to be around Austin. Suddenly the front door opened. Daisy walked with Kelcie and Gia. When Princeton turned Daisy stopped in her tracks. Her face went white like she seen a ghost. Princeton went upstairs to the room he stayed in before. Daisy went upstairs after and in her room. She turned on the music and the girls stayed in her room laughing. He went on Facebook to Rebecca's page and noticed new things were popping up about them, stuff that only Daisy, Kelcie, and Aaron would know.

He peaked out of the bedroom door and noticed Daisy walking to the bathroom. He tip toed out the room and followed her to the bathroom. Once she was in, he closed the door behind him.

"I know it you Daisy. You're the only one that know shit, that we never spoke about around other people. If you were going to pulled something like that, you could be a little more creative."

"Get out Princeton. I shouldn't even be talking to you."

"Then tell me why you made a fake page."

"GET OUT!!!"

"Fine, If you want to expose us and spread rumors then I'll do the same to you. Daisy, I'll tell you one thing…. Don't throw the same dirt, that you dug in also, cause you ain't doing nothing but opening a hole for someone to expose you too." Princeton walked out, leaving

Daisy to think that her plan of exposer to cause drama backfired.

Now she's going to have to come up with something new.

Chapter 17

Princeton has been sitting on the couch waiting for Joey to stop by. He kept looking at his phone hoping he would say he's here. Daisy came downstairs. She looked at Princeton and he looked at her in disgust. She continued to walk to the kitchen with her head down. Princeton got a text saying Joey was on his way. *Thank god.* He thought to himself. He went upstairs to tell his mom he was leaving. He gave her a hug and kissed her the cheek. She started to cry but he told her he will be back when they move.

Princeton got another text message saying Joey is here. He grabbed the bag of the stuff he packed last night and rush downstairs.

"It's sad that your running back to your bitch and not staying with your mom." Daisy said with a smart remark.

"What's sad is you becoming friends with Aaron's side chick." Then Princeton walked out the door. Leaving Daisy standing in silence.

He jumped in the car and they all went back to Joey's. The ride back was quiet. No one said a word, Joey wasn't happy about the visit, but he was relieved. He went to his room and slammed the door behind him. Alani went to her room with her head down, while Princeton followed behind her. He closed the door behind him and sat on the bed with her.

"How'd it go?" Asked Princeton.

"It was good, until he found out about the birth control pills. Then I had to tell him."

"Wait, you're on birth control?"

"Yeah, my aunt Candice made me take them after she found out about that night."

"Damn, no wonder he's pissed. Even if you were pregnant, I try my hardest to prove to your dad I can be a good provider."

"Why prove to my dad? You should prove to me."

"Because I tell you dad not going to make it easy for me just because I'm Austin's nephew."

"Yeah, I can see that."

"I found out who was Rebecca, It's Daisy."

"Daisy?"

"Yeah, I seen the page and I noticed she only posting stuff that we only know. The first day I came down here, she told everything that happened with her and what she did. Those same rumors she posted, is what she told me except the sugar baby thing."

"I should have guessed it was her. She done the whole fake page thing before with Gia."

"I can't wait until the Shadaya going to ripped Daisy's head off."

197

"I know. I just hope she don't end up in jail for murder."

Dinnertime came around and everyone sat in silence. They looked at their plates as they were eating. Then Joey broke the silence.

"I'm disappointed in what I found out, but I can't be mad at your aunt for making you take birth control. I just wish ya'll were a little smarter and waited until ya'll older. I should choke you right now, Princeton for even agreeing to touch her. But I need to be adult and tell ya'll that you better thank god there's not a baby on the way because I promise you, that baby is not going to have a father before it's born. Anyway, how did the night go at Austin's?"

"It went ok. I found out that my cousin Daisy is the one who created that fake page. Plus, my parents are moving out of Austin's house cause they found house on the northside of Tampa."

"Oh, where?"

"I don't know exactly, but I was thinking about moving in with them because she said my uncle won't show up there, Now that I think about it, I doubt it because it Austin. I'll just stay here."

"Good, at least you'll be sticking to your word."

Alani looked at both of them and asked, "What word?"

"It's between us, nothing important." Joey waved it off.

Alani wondered if it they formed some secret bond. That why Princeton was able to come back even after what she told Joey. Her phone started to ring, it's Shadaya calling. She jumped up and rushed to her room.

"Hey, what up." Alani answered.

"I heard that Rebecca page got deleted. I think somebody was behind it and I know exactly who it is."

"I know too."

"How do you know."

"Princeton told me; it was Daisy."

"That's who I was thinking. Who outside our circle would know some of that. How's Princeton?"

"He good, he told us his parents are moving to northside of Tampa."

"Really?"

"Yeah, he said he was thinking about moving there, but he knows Austin going to pop up every now and then. He decided he just going to stay here."

"Well that's good. At lest he can stay away from those people. I realized how quick his family can turn on you. I just hope he is who he say he is."

"Yeah."

"Oh yeah how the doctor's visit go?"

"It didn't go as I hope it would."

"Don't tell me your actually pregnant and you just now finding out."

"No, god no. My dad found out about the birth control pills and I had to tell him why I was on them."

"Awe man, I bet he's pissed."

"Yeah."

"I'll call you later, Mr. Handsome just called me."

Alani giggled. "Tell him I said hi."

They both hung up, then Alani went to the living room cause the boys weren't in the kitchen. She sat down next to Princeton and they watched a movie together. Halfway the movie, an explosion happened, shattering windows, and shaking the house. They all got up with ringing ears. Joey jumped up and looked out the broken window. He seen Alani car on fire and called the 911 for the fire department.

"Dad what's going on"

"I need you both to go outside, right now." Joey said urging them out.

Princeton grabbed Alani and they both went outside. Alani seen her car on fire and freaked out. Princeton tried to calm her down. He held her as she cried and moved her away from the flaming car, to keep her from looking at it. Joey came outside and walk over to Alani and Princeton. Joey got a text message on his phone. He looked at it and seen it was from Austin.

Karma a bitch when you try to fuck me over. Now time is ticking, I want the real shit, or you'll be sleeping with Katrina.

Joey called Mikey and he picked up.

"What's up bro." Mikey answered.

"Mikey what the fuck happened, I thought you gave Austin the stuff."

"I did, what happened now?"

"He just blew up Alani car."

"Shit. I might have gave him the wrong oil cause I only seen one set in the cabinet."

"You only seen one. There should been two, one decoy and the real one."

"I only seen one set. Someone must have taken it."

Joey took a moment to think. The last person that was in the cabinet was Felix.

"I'll call you back." Joey hung up and called Felix. The phone rang until it went to voicemail. Then he called again...no answer. He called for the third time and it wen straight to voicemail. Joey ended up calling Byron.

"Hey, what up?" Said Byron.

"Have you heard from Felix?"

"No, man I haven't. I tried calling him the other day and his phone kept going to voicemail. What's going on?"

"There's been a fuck up with Austin and now I'm in some deep shit."

"Damn, I was going to stop by his house tomorrow. I'll let you know if I talked to him."

"Ok." Joey hung up and sat on the curb and watch the firefighters put out the flame. New Year's is two days away and things are starting to go downhill.

Chapter 18

It's New Year's Eve and nighttime falls, everyone is preparing to celebrate it. There's one place to go and that's to Hotspot for the adults. Since the trio can't go back after the shooting that happened days ago, in fear of being caught, Charlie decides to throw a small party for the teens at his house. Alani, Shadaya, and Princeton are getting ready for the party.

"I wish we were going to Hotspot. I heard everyone was going there before the ball drops. Stupid bitch just had to ruin shit. Now I have to be nice to that weirdo."

"Give Charlie a chance Shadaya. You never know if he could be the one." Said Alani smiling.

"Sorry, but Mr. handsome has a better chance than Charlie."

"How long has Charlie been chasing you with heart eyes and flowers?"

"Stop trying to make it happen Alani."

"Ok, I'm done."

Joey left his car with Alani in case she needed it, while he went to the New Years party with Mikey at Hotspot. They all jumped in the car and headed over to Charlie's. When they got there, the house is packed. It got to the point where people started sitting or standing outside and had the speakers playing the music loudly outside. The trio went to the back and found Aaron, Gia, Charlie is sitting over by the firepit.

"What's sup ya'll. Come sit down. Shadaya, I saved you a seat next me." Said Charlie.

Shadaya looked at Alani. Alani mouthed give him a chance. Then Shadaya sat down next to Charlie with a fake smile on her face. Charlie pulled out a grey rectangular box and gave it to Shadaya. She rolled her eyes and opened it. Inside is a silver diamond necklace.

"I thought I upgrade since were older and you're over the flowers." Said Charlie putting his arm around her.

Shadaya eyes grew big. She don't know if she should continue to be nice or give him a chance. Alani who's next to her nudged her and smiled. Shadaya gave her a "really" look, then Alani shrug saying, "why not."

"Thanks, I love it. You're so sweet." Said Shadaya patting him on the shoulder. "Oh, by the way Aaron, where's Daisy and Kelcie. It's interesting to see you with Gia….out in the open."

"They went to Hotspot. I didn't want to go cause I thought we would get caught from the other night."

Time started go by and as it got clock got closer to 11:30pm, the party started to die down. By the time 11:50 hit, it was just Charlie, Aaron, Gia, Alani, Princeton, and Shadaya. They watch the countdown on the inflatable screen. The ball slowly drop as time counted down to the last seconds. Midnight hit and the ball has dropped. Alani and

Princeton kissed each other, while Aaron and Gia hid behind the tent, and Charlie grabbed Shadaya by the face and kissed her. Shadaya felt weird about it, but she let it go since she was buzzed. Then she can blame it on the alcohol.

Meanwhile at Hotspot……...

Joey and Mikey were having a good time until they seen Austin. He's in the VIP booth with Devin, Jamie, Candice, and Princeton's parents Dana and Clarence. Their up there popping bottles and celebrating when Austin ended up seeing Joey. He smiled and tapped at his wrist. Joey looked away and continued to enjoy what would be a year of hell for him. He phone started to ring.

"Hello." He answered.

"I need you to meet me in the back." Then they hung up.

Joey waved Mikey over and told him to come with him to the back. Once they got to the back, someone started to whistle. They looked around until they seen someone waving them over. They got closer and notice it's Felix.

"Where the fuck have you been and where's my shit?" Joey said angrily.

"I got it, but hear me out. Ya'll wasn't all for what my brother got, so I pitched him your vape oil." He pulled out the oil and a two duffle bags filled with money. "This is how much he wants to pay for it. I told him Austin wanted it and he said he will handle Austin for you, if you agree to his offer."

Joey and Mikey looked at each other. Then they walked over to the side to discuss things.

"Look man, let's just take this offer. It more than what Austin was going to pay for, and it will get him off our backs…...for good." Said Mikey

"I don't know it sounds risky. I don't even know who Felix's brother is and where he's from."

"Well it's a risk we got to take. Either we take this deal and let them deal with Austin or have Austin on our ass every time he wants something new and quick."

"Alright, let do it."

They walked back to Felix and shook his hand.

"We'll take it." Said Joey.

"Nice, I'll my brother know the deal is done."

Joey and Mikey went back to into Hotspot. Felix got on the phone with his twin brother Alex.

"Hey bro. they agree to your offer. Now you can make your move."

"Good, I'll tell the boys get ready."

Everyone continued to party. Joey and Mikey started to feel good about the deal. They ordered another bottle, popped it opened, and raised their glass with Felix. They cheered to each together. Austin stood and watch everything from VIP. He thought

they were celebration for the New Year, but he has a suspicion that it

has to be something else.

Chapter 19

It's Tuesday afternoon, New Year's Day 2019. Everyone at Joey's house is hungover and hungry. So, Joey decides to cook breakfast for everyone with the help of Alani. As everyone is eating, there's a knock on the door. Joey looks at the surveillance camera on his phone. It's Felix and a mystery guy at the door. Joey tapped on Mikey's shoulder telling him to come with him.

They went downstairs to the side door and let the guys in. They all walked into the finished basement. As they sat down at the round table Felix introduce the mystery guy.

"This is my twin brother Alex. He's came all the way from New York."

"Nice to meet you man, I'm sure you heard about us." Said Joey.

"Yeah, I have. I heard your good people and I heard you have problems with an old friend." Said Alex.

"Old friend? You mean Austin?" Said Joey confused.

"Yeah, you see Austin was an old member of my crew Red Bandits and somehow he disappeared. Next thing I know our little sister tells me she's pregnant with his daughter and that she's moving to Florida. So, I had Felix go down there with her to look for him. Now we know, where he is. And it good you agree to our offer, cause now we have a reason to get rid of the motherfucker."

"I guess we're all on the same page. Right?" Said Mikey chiming in.

"Yeah, we are." Said Joey smiling at Alex.

"So, what's ya'll plan?" Mikey is curious.

"We're just going to give him a surprise. Nothing special." Said Felix.

"We came here to drop you off your payment." Alex put the two duffle bags and small brief case of cash on the table. "In this brief case is a little extra for Austin's location."

"You can keep the extra. We'll give you the location and all his spots for a personal reason." Said Joey giving back the extra back.

"I like you guy's, ya'll some humble people." Said Alex.

"Yeah, we don't like to put money on Austin head cause you'll never know with Austin, he could say one thing and do another." Said Mikey.

"Well since we're still on the same page, I think we should head out now. Nice to meet you guys."

"Nice to meet you too." Said Joey shaking his hand.

The twins left the house and they guys went upstairs. Joey noticed that Princeton and Alani weren't in the kitchen no more, so he rushed to Alani and found her sleeping alone in her bed. Then he checked Princeton's room and seen him passed out in his bed. He thought about loosing up the rules since they been following them. He went to the living room and to chill out, smoke, listened to music with Mikey.

At Candice's house.......

Austin just waking up from last night. He got out of bed to use the bathroom. When he was done, he went downstairs to seen Candice sitting on the couch smoking and drinking.

"How the hell are you still drinking after last night?" Austin sat down next to her.

"I wasn't that drunk last night. I had to drive you home, remember?"

"I don't remember anything from last night."

"You got too drunk and too hype and then you noticed Joey and Mikey with Felix and you got real antsy to where you almost got kicked out the club."

"Now I remember. What were those two fuckers doing with Felix?"

"I don't know. I think it's weird that Felix is back. Didn't you tell him not come back, after he threaten you for thinking that you turned his sister into a heroin addict?"

"Yeah, I did. I'm going to have a talk with those two about that. See what the fuck is going on."

Austin rushed upstairs and took a quick shower. He got dressed and got on the phone with Devin. He told him to call Jamie and they meet at Joey's. he threw on his sweatshirt and grabbed his keys.

"Where you going?" Asked Candice.

"I'm going to Joey's and figure this shit out."

"Can I go? I want to see my niece."

Austin sigh and rolled his eyes. "Hurry up, we're running on my time."

Candice rushed upstairs, got dressed and ran back downstairs. They both rushed out and got in the car. On the drive there, Candice tried holding Austin's hand, but he kept snatching it away.

"You know don't like hand holding." Said Austin in a annoyed voice.

"Sorry shit, You can at least be a little romantic."

"Do I look like Romeo to you bitch? Shut the fuck up or will leave your ass on the highway."

Candice rolled her eyes and kept her mouth closed. Once they arrived, he seen Devin car hidden by the tress at the end of the road. Devin and Jamie jumped in Austin's car and they drove up the road to

Joey's house. They all got out and Austin knocked on the side door. They waited until Joey answered the door.

"What's up?" Said Joey unenthusiastic.

"We need to have a talk." Austin pushed the door opened and walked in. Everyone behind him followed.

Mikey came downstairs and they all walked to the finished basement except Candice. She went straight upstairs to find Alani. The guys sat at the table and Austin got straight to the point.

"So, what's going on with ya'll and Felix?" Austin asked curiously.

"Nothing much, he wanted to chill with us one day. So, we made him a part of our crew." Answered Mikey nonchalant.

"Hmm, interesting."

"What are you really here for Austin?" Asked Joey.

"I figured, since Felix is back around, you must have something new coming from him. Like a new product you're not telling me about?"

"Yeah, something new we agreed on. It's this new weed his brother wanted to sell and what it called Joey? Rainbow Dust or something?"

Joey went along with the lie. "Rainbow Daze. He said it will have you seeing shit in different colors."

"Yeah, we just made a deal with him." Said Mikey.

"So, ya'll just gonna make deals without me knowing about it." Said Austin getting angry.

"Sorry man, we thought you cut ties with us because of what happened six years ago." Said Mikey.

"Not anymore, ya'll still owe me some oil. Since I'm here, where's my shit?"

219

"It got stolen, we think it might have been…..."

"WHAT THE FUCK YOU MEAN IT'S STOLEN!!!!?"
Austin jumped up from his chair in anger.

"Somebody broke into Mikey's car and took it." Said Joey
with a quick excuse.

Austin tried to calm down and sat back in the chair.

"You better find out who stole it or make me some new shit.
I'm giving you two weeks. If I don't have by the next two weeks,
then I will have your asses first on my hit list. And I'm make sure
this time, you're gone for good."

Austin got up and walked out with Devin and Jamie behind
him.

"CANDICE WE'RE OUT OR I'MA LEAVE YOUR ASS
HERE.!!!" Austin shouted.

Candice quickly came down the steps and followed Austin out the door with the others with her head down.

Austin lifted her head with his finger. "I'm sorry babe, when there's something suspicious going on, I don't have time to be romantic. To be fair, I'll do whatever you want."

"I can go for some romance."

"Uuuhhh Ok?"

Candice skipped to the car with a smile on face.

"Bro, why do you keep her around if you don't want her?" Asked Devin laughing.

"She can keep tabs on those two and get back to me with their moves." Austin answered.

"Whatever man, As long as it keep us ahead."

They all got in the car and drove back to the northside of Tampa. After they left, Joey and Mikey went back upstairs to chill and jam out to the music.

"I wonder who else is going to pop up today." Said Mikey.

"I hope nobody else. Hopefully, Felix and Alex can come up with a plan before Austin come for our ass."

Chapter 20

Daisy woke up to Kelcie knocking on her bedroom door. She got up and let her in.

"What is it Kels?" Asked Daisy in a sleepy voice.

"Look at this." Said Kelcie handing Daisy her phone.

On Kelcie's Facebook timeline is a selfie that Charlie posted of Charlie with Shadaya behind him smiling, Gia on Aaron's lap while he holding her and Alani with Princeton arm around her shoulder and kissing her cheek while she smiled. The said: *(Ringing in the New Year with the real ones)*. Daisy handed Kelcie the phone as she stared at the wall. The anger rushed through Daisy and she exploded. Stuff started flying around her room as Kelcie sat in silence. Then she sat on her bed and cried.

"To be honest Daisy, it time for you to let go of Aaron."

"I can't we been through so much together and there was times we he been there for me when I needed him the most."

"Yeah, then once he know you're ok, he runs back to Gia until you need him again. Daisy, time doesn't matter, is the respect that he gives you is what matter. As long as he's Charlie and Princeton's friend, he not going drop them for you. Guys like Aaron show more loyalty to each other than their own woman."

"I guess I should."

Daisy picked up her phone and texted Aaron.

I saw Charlie's post. You said you weren't coming with us, but you end up going to Charlie's house. And don't lie cause I have proof you were there.

Five minutes later Aaron texted back: *Charlie called me and wanted me to come. So, I went. I can't say no to him and Gia was already there, cause everybody came to Charlie's before they went to Hotspot. Plus, the whole lap things was nothing really, we all were just messing around.*

Daisy showed Kelcie the message.

"Get rid of him." She said.

Daisy wanted to cry, but Kelcie urged her to do it.

Aaron, I think we should break up. Obviously, you pick Gia over me. You say one thing then you do another. I can't be in this relationship anymore if you keep going back and forth between me and Gia then she can have you.

An hour later Aaron: *If that how you really feel, then I guess, it's whatever.*

Daisy sat there in shock. She thought it will make him want to drop everything for her, but Kelcie was right. He rather choose his friends over her. Realizing that, the sadness turned to back to anger. She rushed to Austin's room and pulled open the drawer filled with guns. She grabbed a .45 caliber with the silencer attached. Next, she grabbed the box with the bullets and then loaded up the gun. She went back to her room and put the safety on and stuffed it in her bookbag.

"What you doing with that?" Asked Kelcie nervously.

"I got something planned for him and everyone else got something coming for them." Said Daisy with a devilish smile.

At Burger World.......

Everyone met up later in the day, after Aaron sent out a group message to everyone about what happened this morning. He walked in seeing, Charlie, Princeton, Alani and Shadaya.

"What's going on bro?" Asked Charlie.

"Man, Daisy just broke up with me this morning." Aaron said sitting down.

"Whaaat." They all said.

"Why she break up with you?" Asked Princeton.

"Cause she saw Charlie's post and got upset cause Gia was on my lap."

"I don't why, ain't she cool with Gia?"

"I don't know, but you what I'm glad she dumped me because she's been acting weird lately. Like she started being friends with Gia, then she dissing Alani and Shadaya, and then she wanted me to drop everybody and just be with her. Like I don't know what going on with her and now she dumped me. I don't know what's going on, but something not right with her."

"Sounds like Daisy going through her bi-polar phase again." Said Shadaya rolling her eyes.

After their conversation, they all decide to hang out at the at Charlie's house. They sat in the backyard and chilled out with a movie playing on the inflatable screen. Then Aaron gets a call from Gia's sister.

"What's up." Aaron answered. He got and went in the house. Five minutes later he tells everybody he got to go.

"You coming back?" Asked Charlie.

"I don't know I got a call from Gia's sister Ali. She said Gia been shot and she in the hospital."

"Ok bro. Let me know what's up."

"Sounds like someone on a rampage. Who else would hate Gia other than Daisy." Shadaya said with an assumption.

"Hey Charlie, where's your bathroom?" Alani asked getting up.

"It's down the hall, straight back."

Alani walked past the front door and notice Aaron falling in bleeding. She screamed and tried to help him up the steps. The rest of the crew came rushing in.

"What fuck happened?" Said Charlie in a panic.

Princeton rush over to help Alani put Aaron on couch.

"I don't know, all I did was walk outside to wait for a ride and somebody with a mask on pulled up and shot me."

Alani called 911 and they waited for he ambulance to come. Then Alani, Princeton and Shadaya got a group text message from an unknown number saying: *YOU'RE NEXT.* Then that's when the fear set in.

Once the ambulance came and got Aaron. Everyone went home. Joey wasn't in the house, so Alani and Princeton decided to take a shower together to wash off the blood and to hold Alani as she cried out of fear. Once they were done, they got dressed and sat in the couch cuddling. An hour later, Joey came in. He noticed Princeton wiping the tears on her face.

"What happened?" Joey asked out of concern.

"We were hanging out at Charlie's and Aaron got shot." Princeton answered.

"How the fuck that happened."

"I don't know, he said he walked outside and waited for a ride and someone pulled up and shot him. Then me, Alani, and Shadaya got a text message saying we're next."

Joey walked away calling Mikey.

"What's going on?" Mikey answered.

"Yo, somebody after Alani."

"Someone after her? What you mean?"

"Princeton just told me Aaron got shot, then him and Alani got a text message saying their next. I don't know what going on, but I think it got Austin written all over it."

"Yeah, we do owe him some oil, or it could be his crazy ass daughter. Remember she try to shoot Alani, but Princeton ended up getting shot."

"Yeah, it could be her. Cause if it is her, shit going to be real bad. Cause nobody going to hurt my daughter."

"True. Why don't you have a talk with Princeton."

"About what?"

"See what lead up to this then figure out after that."

"I see what you mean. I'll call you back and let you know."

"Aight."

They both hung up and Joey seen Princeton door cracked open and the lights are on. He knocked on the door and walked in.

"We need to talk about today." Said Joey as he sat down on the edge of the bed.

"Sure."

"So, how did the day start?"

"It started when we all met at Burger World cause Aaron sent us a text. He told us that Daisy broke up with him. Cause she seen a picture of Gia sitting on Aaron's lap. Then we went to Charlie's to hang out and Aaron got a call saying that his friend Gia got shot. So, he went outside to wait for a ride, and he ended up getting shot. Honestly, I think it was Daisy that shot both of them or she had someone do it for her. Cause there's no reason for both Aaron and Gia to get shot after Daisy broke up with him."

"Yeah that makes sense. Well if you get anything new that pops up, let me know."

"Ok."

Joey walked out of the room. He scroll through his contacts and texted Felix.

Hey whatever plan you got with Austin, I want in. My daughter been threatened by his. Now it's war.

Felix texted back: *Sure, I'll let my brother know. He will be glad to have someone keep close tabs on Austin.*

An hour later Felix sent out another text message: *My brother said will meet you at your house Friday and expect more guys with him.*

Joey texted Mikey: *I'm sorry man, but I figure out who it that threaten Alani. It's Austin daughter Daisy, Princeton said she shot their friend Aaron and his friend Gia. Then I figured she the one that sent threating texts to him, Alani, and her friend. Talking about their next. So, I asked Felix, whatever plan they have with Austin. I want in, it war about my daughter's life. They want to come to my house to meet Friday.*

Mikey text back: *Hey if you're in, I'm in. I just hope it not a bunch of bullshit. But at least we won't have to worry about Austin, plus I always got your back.*

Thanks man.

No problem, you're my bro and she's my niece. If you're fighting, I'm fighting.

Chapter 21

It's been two days since they last heard about Daisy. She hasn't even shown up to school yet. Everyone think that she's hiding out after those two shootings that happened. Aaron is at home recovering and Gia is in critical condition and doctors say she may not make it. Down at Joey's house. Joey, Mikey, And Byron are in the finished basement getting ready for this meeting. Five minutes later, there's a knock on the door. Joey got to answer it, then he came back with a group of six guys.

"I would like for you to meet these four guys. Korey, Lucas, Carlos, and Juan." Felix introduced.

"Nice to meet ya'll. This is Mikey and Byron; they are a part of my crew. And I'm Joey." Joey introduced shaking hands.

They all sat down at the table. Felix handed Joey a paper with the hitlist of the names. On there, is Austin and the people who are associated with him. A couple of people were marked in red showing that their the one to kill on sight. Candice name is on there, but she's written in black meaning on watch.

"That's the list of people we been watching keeping tabs on everyone. Your name was list, but I took you guys off since we made a deal. Also, here's the times and places, ya'll gave us. We marked the ones where he would be there the most. So, we have to get him in places where he don't be at. That way we can catch him off guard." Alex explained.

"Damn, ya'll know how to stay ahead a person who's unpredictable." Said Mikey impressed.

"Hey, we learned how to move like him by watching him." Said Alex. "We were going to start setting up and getting ready for these hits, but now we got to switch up some things. Now that got more people, we can cover more ground. Me, Felix, and Byron will take northside, Carlos and Lucas will take southside, Korey and Juan will take westside, and You and Mikey take eastside. Everybody cool with that?" Said Alex laying out the plan.

Everyone shook their head in agreement.

"Best to do this is at night. It will be easier to stay hidden and keep track. Drop a pin on the location and if he moves let us know, then follow him. If he the location someone else is in, then let them know and drop a pin on that location for the others and they will move the same."

"When we doing this?" Asked Joey

"What days does Austin move the most at night?"

"Fridays, Saturdays, and Wednesdays. Saturday is when he's most active. It's the weekend and that's when he sells the most." Said Byron.

"Cool, then we could catch him next Saturday. Joey you ok with us meeting here?"

"Yeah, it's cool. What time?"

"5pm, we'll go the plan again and more, then we'll head out at 6pm. I need everybody to drive around their location, get familiar and then get into place once the sun drops."

They all agreed, got up and shook hands. Then the guys headed out. Once Felix and his crew left, The three guys went upstairs to chill out, smoke, drink and listen to some music. They cheered each other and jammed out the music. An hour later, Alani, Princeton and Shadaya came up the steps.

"What going on dad?" Alani asked.

"Nothing much, we're just hanging out." Answered Joey.

"Ok."

The trio headed of to Alani's room.

"So, what are you going to do about Austin's daughter after we're done with Austin?" Mikey wondered.

"I'll have Princeton handle that. It's his family and it's personal." Said Joey.

"Why don't you call him in here and we'll have a talk with him." Said Byron.

"I'll see if he wants to."

Joey got up and walk to Alani room. He cracked the door open and peaked his head in.

"Hey Princeton, come hang with the boys for a minute." Joey closed the and walked away. Princeton looked at Alani.

"Go ahead, I seems like you not in trouble." Said Alani smiling.

"Yeah, go spend some time with your father-in-law." Said Shadaya.

239

Then they both laughed. Princeton smiled, threw a pillow at Shadaya, and walked out.

Princeton walked into the living room.

"Heey." They all said.

"Come sit with us. Have a drink." Said Byron passing a cup to Princeton.

Joey snatched the cup from Byron. "Whoa man, he's a kid. Anyway, we wanted to talk to you about something. This is between us; you can't tell Alani." Said Joey with a serious look.

"Ok, what you need me to do."

"I need you to handle Daisy."

"Don't worry, Charlie will be with you for safety." Mikey jumped in.

"How do you want me to handle her?" Princeton asked.

"Whatever you want. Let her know if she fuck with Alani, she got to get through you first. Kinda like how you did Austin." Said Joey.

"Ok, When do you want me to do this?"

"Whenever you want day you want. We have mission for Austin, and we need her to bring him to us in case he runs."

"Alright, I can plan something out with Charlie tomorrow and keep it a secret."

"Good, I'm starting to like you more kid." Said Joey putting his arm around Princeton.

"Hey, anything to protect Alani, like I promised her."

"That a boy." Said Mikey patting him on the shoulder.

"You don't need to be with the girls anyways. Stay out here and hang with us men." Said Byron.

Byron handed Joey a cup half full Hennessey and a blunt. Then Joey took a puff and passed it Princeton with the cup of Hennessey.

"Since we're keeping secrets, here, I'll let this slide." Joey smiled and winked at Princeton.

Princeton took the cup and blunt and smiled back. He's glad he could gain Joey's trust. He thinks he maybe starting to have a bond with Joey, or that thought could be too soon. The guys hung around, laughed, and was having a good time. Alani wondered what was taking Princeton so long to come. Her and Shadaya decide to take a peak quietly at what was going on. Alani seen Princeton smiling with her dad and laughing with the guys. She look at Shadaya who mouthed two months and tapped her ring finger. They both giggled quietly, and tip toed back to her room.

Chapter 22

Princeton texted Charlie to see if he had time today to hang. Once he got the text back saying yeah. He jumped in the shower, got dressed and He told Alani he is going to Charlie's and her kissed good-bye. He got a Uber to Charlie's to house and when he arrived there, he texted Charlie saying he is here.

"What's up man." Said Charlie at the door.

"Hey bro."

Charlie let Princeton in, and they headed off to his room. They sat on the futon and Charlie grabbed his weed tray and started rolling a blunt.

"You talk to you uncle yet?" Princeton asked.

"Yeah yesterday. He told me about them wanted you handing Daisy. How do they know it's Daisy that been shooting and threating everybody?"

"I told Joey what happened. And I guess he put everything together from Aaron getting shot to that night at Hotspot."

"What happened at Hotspot?"

"Shadaya and Daisy got into it then Kelcie and Shadaya. Then Daisy and Alani. All of sudden Daisy tried to shoot Alani, but I Jumped in front of her and ended up getting shot. And then Daisy and Aaron was fighting over a gun and fired more shots."

"Oh, that was that night everybody was talking about and posting on Facebook. Damn that was ya'll?"

"Yeah. Now they think the threats are coming from Daisy. Because they think she's the one that shot Aaron and Gia."

"Yeah, that would make sense. You know Gia died yesterday."

"Really when she die?"

"It was like around 3 in the afternoon. Yeah, Aaron called me and told me. I told him if he wanted to come over and talk, I'll be here all day. I know he's fucked up in the head right now. Even though he shouldn't have been cheating with Gia, he was real chill with her. He seem annoyed with Daisy. The only reason why he stayed with her is cause he works for her dad."

"Yeah, I used to be on edge with Alani's dad, but after last night, he seem cool with me. I might gain his trust. He even trust me to get rid of Daisy."

"That's what sup. That's good man, he might even get you to do moves for him."

"Nah I doubt it. Alani wouldn't allow that. The only way for me to convince her to let me to make moves, is to have her dad do it."

Charlie got a text message from Aaron saying he's here. So, Charlie went downstairs and came back up with him.

"What's up, you alright?" Asked Princeton

245

"Yeah, I'm ok." Said Aaron looking down with sadness.

"So, what the plan Princeton?" Asked Charlie.

"Plan? What plan?" Aaron included himself.

"Alani's dad wants Princeton to get rid of Daisy."

"Well whatever the plan is, I'm in."

Charlie and Princeton looked at Aaron in shock.

"You sure?" asked Princeton still in shock.

"Yeah, so what's the plan?"

"Well, I haven't thought of one, but I think we should do a kidnapping or at least threaten her back with some messages."

"I pick the kidnapping. Then beat her ass until she has enough suffering, then shoot her in the head." Said Charlie coming up with something.

"I think we should do just the kidnapping and see what we should do next." Said Princeton suggested something else.

"Why? We need to get rid of her for good. If she's able to shoot me and Gia, who know what else she got planned for ya'll." Said Aaron.

"If my uncle find out he's going to go nuts. So, we have to do this without being suspicious. We can't tell nobody not even Alani."

"Why can't we tell her?" Asked Aaron.

"Cause, if she's finds out her dad wants me to this. She going to think I'm making moves for her dad and think I'm into some deep shit I can't get out of."

"What we going to do?" Charlie wondered.

They sat around and thought for a moment. Then Aaron came up with something.

"I still got Daisy's number. Let just buy a burner phone, make her think it her think it's mom. Then have her meet us somewhere at night where there's less people and snatch her up in a rental."

"How we going to get a rental? And what if Austin finds out that Daisy missing?"

"I can call my cousin from New York and see if he can come down here and get us a rental and have a few of his people deal with Austin." Said Aaron.

Aaron texted his cousin and as they waited, they passed around the blunt. Then he got a message back. He looked at the phone confused and texted his cousin back. Then he got a message back and then a lightbulb went off.

"What he say?" Asked Charlie.

"He said he already down here and they got a meeting planned with Austin next week. He said he can get us a rental, but I had to tell him why." Then Aaron got another message. "He said hold off on the plan, we can use that for next week. He has to let Joey know what new?"

"Joey? I wonder if he's talking about Alani's dad. I don't know if that was a good idea to tell him." Said Princeton worried.

"Well I can't keep secrets from my cousin. His head boss is gonna want to know what's up. You can't be secretive with Red Bandits. They won't hesitate to kill you if they think your being suspicious."

"Wait, you cousin with the Red Bandits?" Said Princeton in shock.

"Yeah, why?"

"I know them. My dad and my uncle used to work for them. Shit, they're in town?"

"Yeah, that what he said."

"I got to call Alani and see if she's home and have her put her dad on the phone." Princeton jumped up and rushed out the room.

"I thinking I might have to strap up, cause shits about to get real." Said Charlie lighting the blunt.

At Joey's………..

Alani came in Joey's room and gave him her phone.

"Princeton wants to talk to you."

Joey took the phone. "Yeah."

"You might get a call from someone in Red Bandits."

"Why?" He noticed Alani standing by the door and waved her off. She rolled her eyes and went back to her room.

"I told Charlie what was going on and we were coming up with plan, then Aaron came and found out, so I told him and he now he's all in. So, he called his told him what was going on because we needed a rental."

"Why didn't you ask me to get you one?"

"Because I thought you wouldn't wanted in your name."

"Next time ask me first before you start putting shit into action. How the hell you know I had contact with Red Bandits?"

"They mentioned your name. We had to tell them after that because they suspect something, your gonna die, they won't care if your innocent. Those are dangerous people. That why my uncle and dad are here and hiding out. Cause my uncle did a lot of sneaky things behind their back and they didn't like that. So, they came after my dad. Just so that my uncle can come to them."

"No wonder why they came down here. Someone must have told them Austin lives here."

"Well I just called to give you heads up."

"Aight, thanks letting me know."

"You're welcome."

They both hung up. Joey got up and went to Alani's room. He walked in and handed back her phone.

"What going on dad? Why did Princeton want to talk to you?"

"It nothing, just something with Austin came up." Joey lied.

"What happened?"

"Alani it's nothing for you know."

"What's really going on dad? You and Princeton been having this secret bond and then ya'll not even telling me anything. I don't like this. I'm starting to think you have Princeton working for you."

"Alani, this is street stuff you don't need to know. I don't need you involved in this."

"Just tell me what's going on. I feel like something bad is going to happened."

"Nothing is going to happen. Everything going to be fine."

"I remember the last time somebody said that to me, and something went wrong where somebody gets shot."

"Hey shit happens but were just trying to protect you from that. Plus, we're trying to get rid of Austin, so he doesn't get us into more shit."

"Ok."

Joey walked out the room. Alani texted Princeton: *What's going on?*

He texted her back: *I can't tell you; I promise your dad I wouldn't tell you anything. It will be ok Alani. I need you to still trust me on my word. This is just to keep you out of harm's way.*

"I don't need protecting. I need someone who's not going to keep secrets from me and tell me what's going on. Whenever I'm left in the

dark, I always think something is happing and I ended up going to

lose you or my dad. I don't want to lose neither of you.

Do you need me to come home?

Yeah, I feel like something going to happen. I'm getting

nervous, especially if you're not telling me things.

Ok I'll be on my way.

Alani put her phone and laid on the bed. Two hours later,

Princeton walks in her room. He walked over to her and gave her

a hug.

"Even if someone were to hurt you, they know the

consequences. It will end up being a death sentence for them."

Alani looked up at Princeton. He smiled and gave her a kiss.

Alani felt a little better, but it didn't calm her enough to know

things would be ok.

Chapter 23

It's the day before the big mission with the boys. Alex got the boys their rental and he also brought the burner phones they wanted. The boys met up at Charlie's house to go over the plan. Aaron searched through his phone for Daisy's number. Then he started to write up a text.

Hey princess, this mommy. I just got out of rehab and I want to see you. Meet me at Burger World at 8pm. I'll be behind it because I don't want your father to know I'm released. I love you honey, can't wait to see you.

The boys sat around and wait to see if Daisy would take the bait. Half hour later, a message comes through.

Sure, mom I'll meet you around then.

Eight o'clock comes around and the boys wait for Daisy to stop by their way. The street behind is dark and no one likes being back here cause of how dark it is. Ten minutes later, Daisy walks up the street. She stops by the back door of the building. Aaron slowly creep out of the bushes and quickly place a bag over her head. He wrestles with until Charlie ran up and grabbed her legs. They carry her and threw her in the trunk. They jump in and Princeton drives off.

They pull up to an abandon building two blocks from Imes Church. It used to be an old gentlemen's club called Blackberries. Princeton pulls around to the back. He back up towards the back door and parks. Aaron and Charlie grabbed Daisy out of the trunk and handcuff her to the bars of the cage.

"Good job boys." A man appears from the dark.

"Alex?"

"Hey Princeton, been a while since I seen you." Said Alex.

"Yeah." They gave each other a hug.

Daisy started fidgeting and mumbling under the bag. Alex removed the bag from Daisy head and her eyes widened.

"Hey niece, I see your dad took care of you, of course."

"Fuck you, when he finds out I'm missing, he's going to raise hell."

"Well we got something for him coming. So, he can raise hell if he wants to." Said Alex nonchalant.

Alex closed the cage shut, put a pad lock on it and walked away. Daisy look over at the boys and smiled.

"Ya'll think this is supposed to scare me." She laughed. "I got my dad something he always wanted. Joey going to come home with one less person."

"What did you do?" Princeton charged at the cage and shook it.

"We pretty much took her and gave her to my dad. Who knows what he's doing with her right now."

257

"Where is she Daisy?"

"Can't tell you."

"DAISY!!!!"

Daisy sat in silence. She stared at Princeton with a smile on her face and started running her hand across the bars and humming. Princeton got upset and walked out, then the boys followed him after. Aaron dropped off Charlie first, then Princeton last. Princeton rushed upstairs and into Alani's room. Joey is sitting on the bed with his face buried in his hands.

"What going to happen now?" Princeton asked.

Joey looked up and gazed out the open window.

"I'm waiting on Alex for the next move. He thinks Austin knows about Red Bandits being here."

Joey phone went off and it's a call from Alex.

"What's up?" Joey answered.

"Scrap the plans, Austin knows. He wants us to meet him at Blackberries tomorrow at 8pm."

"Shit, ok. I wonder who the hell told him."

"I don't know, but somebody in your circle gave him information.

At Austin's………

Austin sat in his room with Alani handcuffed to his bed. Alani started to wake up after being passed out from a cloth soaked with chloroform. Austin looked over and smile.

"Look who's awake."

Alani looked around in fear. She tried to jumped out the bed, but she quickly realized she's handcuffed.

"Where you going? You don't want to spend some time with me."

Alani sat there in silence. She put her head down to avoid looking at Austin.

"Awe babygirl don't look so sad. We'll have a good time, I promise."

"I doubt it. My dad and Princeton probably wondering where I am and come looking for me. And they'll find me."

"Hmmm, I doubt it. See they can look all over the city, but I got people who can move you around and keep you out of sight."

"Don't get too happy. You keeping me hostage isn't last long."

Austin laid down next to Alani and start to touch her cheek softly.

"I'm not going to worry, I still got time."

He pushed Alani down the bed and got on top of her. He covered her mouth with his hand.

"Now we going to have some fun. I ain't forget my word six years ago.

Chapter 24

It's Saturday night and eight o'clock comes around. Joey and the boys arrived at Blackberries. They all got out and walked in. The light in the room was dim and there's not a person in sight. Princeton looked at the cage and seen it was empty. Suddenly Austin walks in with a smile on his face.

"What a hell of a reunion." Austin said.

"Cut the shit Austin, you know we here for unfinished business." Alex said in a stern voice.

"Where's Alani? I know you got her." Said Joey in an angry voice.

"She fine, she's in the back. PRINCESS, BRING OUT ALNAI!!!"

Daisy came out with Alani with her hands tied up and a with a scarf wrapped around her mouth. She is in tears and wearing Austin sweatpants and tee shirt and her hair is in a mess.

"What the fuck you do to my daughter. I swear if you did anything to her, I will end your fucking life." Said Joey with an angry threat.

Felix held back Joey and Austin smiled.

"Oh, we just had a little fun. Right Alani?" Said Austin petting her head then pulling her hair.

Alani shook her head saying yes still crying. Austin kissed her head and threw her on the floor. Princeton quickly grabbed they gun out of his pocket and aim it at Austin. Mikey snatched it away as he looked around. He knew there's people hiding out somewhere cause Austin done it before.

"Let the boy shoot me Mikey. Since he had the balls to threaten me before. I bet you been waiting for that moment to shoot me, huh Princeton."

Princeton can feel his body shake in anger.

"Austin your times up." Said Alex.

"You sure."

Five shots rang out. Juan and Lucas goes down. A few more shots rang out and Carlos goes down. Appearing from the dark behind Joey and the boys is Devin and Jamie. They both stood behind them.

"How did know we were here?" Asked Alex.

"A little birdie in your circle told me." Said Austin smiling. "Thanks for the info Byron. You been a big help."

Then Austin shot him, hitting him in the chest. Alani is still on the floor crying until Daisy kicked her in the head. Princeton ran over, grabbed by the neck, and started to choke her. Aaron ran over, grabbed

Princeton, and dragged him away from her. Breaking away from Aaron's grip, Princeton ran over to Alani. He tried to untie her, but Daisy put a gun to his head.

"Don't even think about it." Said Daisy.

"Fuck you Daisy."

Princeton got up and punched her. He took the gun away from her and shot her in the head. Everyone stopped and stood there in shock.

"You little shit." Austin ran over with tears filling up his eyes. "Daisy......Princess." No response, blood started to drip from her head and her mouth. Austin screamed he took out his gun and aimed at Princeton. Before he can even pull the trigger, Alani swings her legs around tripping Austin, which gave Joey time to run over and he points the gun at Austin.

"It's over Austin." Then Joey fired shots until Austin stopped moving.

Both Jamie and Devin started shooting. Princeton untied Alani and ran outside to get her to safety.

Felix ended up getting Jamie. Korey was got shot in the chest from Devin. As Devin tried to run, Mikey shot him in the back. Then he walked up to Devin and fired two shots in his head. Once the gun smoke cleared, Joey, Mikey, Felix, Alex looked around.

"I guess were done here." Said Alex.

As Felix and Alex went to leave, A couple shots rang out. The guys stopped and started shooting back. Then they heard Felix screamed, he was on the ground with a bullet wound in his leg. The shooter stopped and it got silent. Confused, they started to look around.

Then Aaron walked up and fired two shots at Felix in the head and ran off. Alex ran over to his brother and held him. Then he got up and started looking for Aaron. When he spotted him in an empty room, He ran inside and ended up getting shot by Clarence, who was watching Alani before Daisy came and got her.

After hearing the shots from the other room, Joey and Mikey ran off. They jumped in the car and took off. With Princeton and Alani in the backseat, they all headed off to Joey's house. When they got there, everyone went into their rooms. Princeton is allowed to sleep in Alani's room, so that Mikey can sleep in his. Princeton grabbed all his stuff out of there and brought it to Alani room. Joey and Mikey sat in the living room and started smoking and drinking.

"I'm glad shits over." Joey taking shots.

"I doubt it. Don't forget about Candice, once she finds out, she's going to be pissed. Plus, his brother moved here, so we don't know where he is. We going to have to make a quick move. Maybe start over somewhere else."

"Yeah."

After they got done chilling, smoking, and drinking they both went to bed. Around one in the morning, Princeton woke up to the sound of his phone ringing. It was Dana calling him. He got up and quietly went to the downstairs bathroom.

"Hello." He answered in quiet voice.

"Princeton, where are you? Your uncle and you cousin are dead, and your father sitting here wondering where you are."

"I can't tell you mom, I'm somewhere where we have to stay hidden."

"Well, be careful because someone…."

Princeton heard Dana scream on the phone, then gunshots.

"Mom." Princeton voice cracked.

Tears started rolling down his face. Then a voice said……

"Thanks for getting rid of my boyfriend and my best friend. The two main people I had in my life that was closes to me. Now you have

267

no parents. Don't think ya'll in the clear because I got something coming you."

"Kelcie?"

Then the phone hung up. Princeton went back upstairs and got back in bed. He couldn't shut his eyes after that call. If it was Kelcie, how did she know about them being dead?

Chapter 25

Five months go by and Alani and Princeton convinced Joey they should move out and take Princeton's parents' house that been brought out. Joey thought it wasn't a good idea, but with the situation they're in, he figured it would be ok space wise. After packing up the moving truck, Alani gave Joey a hug and Joey gave Princeton a side hug.

"Call me when you get there." Said Joey.

"Ok." Said getting in the car.

They drove from Joey house and onto the street where the house is located. As they drove the street, the houses started to look familiar to her. Once they pulled up to the house. It looked kind of like the house Alani used to live, but in a different shade of color. They parked the truck in the walkway to the front door, got out and unlocked the house door. As they both walked in everything in the house was clean. It didn't even look like anybody lived here. They waited for Shadaya and Charlie to come to help unload the truck. Once they arrived, that when the boys started unloading.

"I'm so happy you guys have your own house. No more rules and parties every day."

"Hmm give us a few more months to get comfortable then we can party."

Alani went upstairs to see what it looks like. It's all starting to look familiar, but hasn't it hasn't clicked yet. Shadaya came up stairs with Alani stuff. She noticed Alani standing the room and looking around.

"I'm guessing this is ya'll room?"

"Yeah, this will be our room. Something feels weird about this house."

"What do you mean?"

"I don't know, it feels too familiar." Then she went into the next room and it was padlocked.

She rushed downstairs and asked Princeton do he have the key to the lock on the door upstairs. He gave her the key and she rushed back upstairs. After she unlock the lock, she opened the door. The room walls are white with a table, chair and a door on the wall that look like a safe door. Alani walked over to the safe door and touched it. She tried punching in the code many times. Her last thought was Princeton's birthday. The safe door opens and inside is stacks of money and bricks of cocaine. Her eyes widen and so did Shadaya's when she walked in.

"Holy shit, what ya'll going to do with all of this?" Shadaya Asked.

"I don't know, I would have to ask Princeton, since this is his dad stuff anyway."

Alani and Shadaya went downstairs to start unpacking. Princeton came back upstairs with a pink headboard with flowers on them.

"Look what I found in the basement. I don't know what we could use this for. It's got hinges and a lock on it."

Then it hit her. The safe in the wall use to be a crawl space for Alani when she was nine. And the room she was in before was her mother's room. She sat on the floor with sad look on her face.

"What's wrong Alani?" Asked Shadaya.

"This my old house." She got up and stood in a spot on the two feet from where the tv used to be. "This spot is where my mom died."

Then she sat down and started to cry. Princeton sat on the floor next to her and hugged her.

"It will be ok. We can make new memories here. Hey, I lost my parents here too. But we going to make sure this place is good for our little one on the way. Alani smiled and hugged Princeton. Then Shadaya joined in with Charlie behind her. She gave Charlie the 'don't touch me' look, but he still hugged her anyway.

"I guess we building a whole new family." Said Princeton.

"We're basically family anyway." Then she changed the subject. "Hey Princeton, what are you going to do with those bricks of cocaine that upstairs?"

"Cocaine?"

They all headed upstairs and went into the room where the safe is. Alani opened the safe and Princeton and Charlie eyes got wide.

"Got damn. It's a fortune in here. You should sell it." Said Charlie looking through it.

"Nah, I will give to Alani's dad if he wants it." Said Princeton looking at Alani.

"I don't think he will take it. Why don't we give to Aaron."

"He been MIA lately. I tried calling to see what was up, but I think he changed his number cause it said this number isn't in service." Said Princeton.

"Let just create our own business and sell it discreetly. I mean you going to need the money for your daughter." Shadaya suggested.

"Alright, as long as my dad doesn't find out. He doesn't want us involved in the business anymore."

"Question is, where are we going to sell it?" Princeton asked.

"We'll have to go outside the city." Said Charlie with an idea.

Down at Aaron's house………

Aaron is in his room laying in his bed. He changed his number, cut his hair and clean sweep his friend list on all his social media pages. He was enjoying the quiet time he had until there was a knock on the front door. He got up, grabbed his gun, and went downstairs. He looked out one of the side door windows. It is a female standing there with a hood over her head and glasses.

He opened the door slowly and peaked his head through.

"What you want?"

"It's me Kelcie."

He opened the door wide enough to let her in. They both sat on the couch and Kelcie took off her hood and glasses.

"What bring you here?"

"I heard what happened and I haven't heard much from you. Where have you been?"

"I been here chilling, out of sight. Why, what you up to?"

"Nothing much, I just wanted to call it truce, if we had any beef between us. See I met some new friends and they need a leader for their crew who knows the ins and outs of the game. Since you worked with Austin, you know the products he selling. I already grabbed most of it and showed it to them, they just need someone to show them how push it and where to."

"I don't know about that Kelcie. I want to be out of this shit."

"But look at this way, you won't have to work for anybody, not even for Joey. You can even have the guys scare them out the city and take over. No more Joey, Alani, and Princeton, you won't even worry about them."

"This starting to sound a little personal."

"Nothing personal, Just offering a partnership opportunity, unless you want them to find out who came out alive that night."

"Alright Kelcie, I'll take it."

"Good, I'll let the guys know."

They both got up and walked to the door. They shook hands and Kelcie went on her way. Aaron closed the door and went back to his room. He rolled up a blunt and got comfortable in his bed with the music channel on.

"I guess I'm still working for Austin, Just a female version." He said to himself.

To be continued............

Made in the USA
Monee, IL
10 November 2020

47147321R00153